SCENES FROM ANIMAL LIFE

Scenes From Animal Life

Nine Pairs of Fables for the Enneagram Types

Waltraud Kirschke

*Translated by Sister Isabel Mary SLG
with Illustrations by Dee Lane*

SLG Press
Convent of the Incarnation
Fairacres Oxford

Translated by Sister Isabel Mary SLG from the German
Enneagramms Tierleben: 2 x 9 Fabeln
published 1993 by Claudius Verlag München

© Claudius Verlag München 1993

World English Translation Rights © The Sisters of the Love of God
1998

Illustrations and Cover Picture © Dee Lane 1998

ISBN 0 7283 0149 0
ISSN 0307-1405

Printed by Will Print, Oxford
Bound by Paper Back Binders (Oxford) Ltd, Abingdon

Contents

Preface	vii
Foreword	viii

Type One
Order Is The Most Important Thing In Life	1
Let Your Wings Carry You	6

Type Two
Love Cannot Be Earned	13
It's A Thankless World	19

Type Three
Who Am I Without My Colours?	24
The True Self Is Behind The Facade	30

Type Four
All Animals Are Part Of One Great Unity	35
An Aesthetically Beautiful Death, At Least	41

Type Five
A Detached And Objective View Of The World	46
All Theories Yield To Love	52

Type Six
New Situations Create New Problems	57
The Brave Struggle With Fear	62

Type Seven
Don't Burden Yourself With Negative Thinking	67
Under The Surface Of Life There Are Depths	73

Type Eight

A Soft Heart Under A Thick Skin — 79
Might Is Right — 84

Type Nine

Anything for Peace And Quiet — 89
It Does You Good To Speak Your Mind — 93

Preface

The following animal stories are intended as fables to illustrate the Enneagram. The incentive to write them came from the book by Richard Rohr and Andreas Ebert: *Discovering the Enneagram—an Ancient Tool for a New Spiritual Journey*, in which different animal symbols are assigned to the nine energies.

I was inspired chiefly by the animal stories of Manfred Kyber. His vivid and humorous portrayal gave me a model and encouraged me to feel my way towards the fables and to transpose them into the typology of the Enneagram.

Waltraud Kirschke

Foreword to the German Edition

All cultures of mankind—with the exception of the Euro-American culture of the last two centuries—have retained the knowledge that there is a kind of 'correspondence of energies' between human characteristics and the nature of certain animals. This insight is reflected, for example, in the totemism of the North American Indians, which springs from a deeply reverent accord with nature and regards humans and animals as embodied forms of the one great Spirit. The Bible uses animal symbols, like the snake to indicate the cunning of evil, or the dove as a symbol of purity and of the Spirit. In the Revelation of John, Christ is represented by the paradoxical animal symbols of the lion and the lamb.

This primitive human intuition is reflected in another way in the animal fables of many advanced cultures, which are intended to impart general truths about morality and practical wisdom as a form of instruction or social criticism. The oldest fables are to be found in Sumerian texts of the earlier part of the second millennium BCE. The most famous collection of fables in antiquity dates from the sixth century before Christ and is attributed to Aesop. The fables of the Indian Panchatantra and of Luqman the Arab exerted a great influence on medieval European literature. In the age of the Reformation and again in that of the Enlightenment fables still flourished, only to fade into almost complete oblivion in the present century—apart from the amusing animal stories of Manfred Kyber, George Orwell's *Animal Farm*, Erich Kästner's *Conference of the Animals*, or Rudyard Kipling's

Jungle Book. There are, of course, knowledgeable people who regard cartoon characters such as Mickey Mouse as a continuation of the socially critical fable

The spiritual wisdom of the Enneagram—influenced no doubt by Sufi traditions—teaches that there are nine basic forms of the human character, each with its specific blocks and fixations. It is also part of the oral tradition of the Enneagram that—as well as other symbols such as colour or nationality—specific 'totemic' animals are ascribed to each of the nine fixations. When in everyday speech we refer to someone as a 'bull,' or a 'frightened rabbit,' a 'peacock,' 'turtle-dove,' 'monkey,' or 'timid doe,' we are alluding to the same corresponding energies which are designated in the oral tradition of the Enneagram.

Waltraud Kirschke, a theologian and biologist closely concerned with new ways of Christian thinking, is a foundation member of the Hamburg Centre for Christianity and the Inner Life. She has expanded what in some Enneagram textbooks is merely indicated, by devising a pair of animal fables for each of the nine Enneagram types. Slight and amusing as these stories may appear at first sight, much more lies behind them. They hold up a mirror before us which, if we give it more than a fleeting glance, can cause us pain. But they may also spark off a recognition that enables us to laugh at ourselves. And people who are never able to discover themselves in abstract discussions about the Enneagram may perhaps experience a moment of truth through these stories. I commend them to all readers for pleasure and enlightenment.

Andreas Ebert
(*co-author of* Discovering the Enneagram)

Type One

(i)

Order Is the Most Important Thing in Life

WE MUST have order!' said Carla, as she dragged the raisin destined for the state storage depot straight behind her into the very middle of the ant road. 'Order is the most important thing in life. Take note of that!'

Carla was a large red wood-ant with correctly sitting armour-plating and exemplary feeler-carriage. She was constantly concerned for order in the ant colony and always ready to do her utmost to maintain it—as now, for example.

Behind Carla marched more ants. They were still young and Carla had the responsibility of introducing them to their tasks as workers, for she was a good teacher.

Carla preferred to give practice-orientated instruction. This not only saved time, but also allowed the young ants to make themselves useful immediately, and with this in mind she and her pupils had already spent the whole morning collecting the remains of a picnic in the woods.

There were delicacies such as scraps of fruit, bread-crumbs and raisins—really awkward things and quite difficult to move. But that was no problem for regular worker-ants.

Carla concentrated on the matter in hand and she showed all the ants who had raisins to cope with that the way to transport a raisin was not to carry it or push it (with raisins of this size it was impracticable) but to pull it along behind you.

At last the ants had covered the greater part of the way and it would not be long before they reached their destination, the home ant-hill. But now they had come to a

Type 1

bridge. There was a fir-needle spanning a deep crack in the ground in which rain-water had collected.

'We must have order,' declared Carla, and she proceeded to pull her raisin carefully along the fir-needle.

'Hadn't we better go another way?' asked an ant behind her. 'The bridge is too narrow here but we could find another way round.'

She was a very young ant, hardly beyond the larva stage, and so of course hadn't got the right attitude to order and correct behaviour.

Carla gave her a disapproving look.

'Bridges are there to be crossed,' she said, lifting a feeler, 'and roads are there to be kept to. If we don't cross the bridge we shall lose the road, and that would be wrong.' But to her dismay, the young ant had already turned aside with her load and was crawling along the edge of the crack looking for another way, and all the others who had been following her in single file were doing the same. Some went left, some went right, but not one of them was crossing the bridge.

'Oh, this is absolute chaos!' cried Carla. 'Come back! You're all going the wrong way!'

But seeing that no one was listening to her, she angrily took hold of her raisin and crossed the bridge alone. If all these hopeless scatterbrains went off the track *she* at least would conduct herself in accordance with order and propriety.

Twice she almost fell into the water, but eventually she did get safely to the other side of the crack and hurried off to catch up with her pupils. They, meanwhile, had all got together again, like a river that divides into little streams only to flow once more into a single current.

'It's about time order was restored in this swarm,' muttered Carla crossly, and again she dragged her raisin

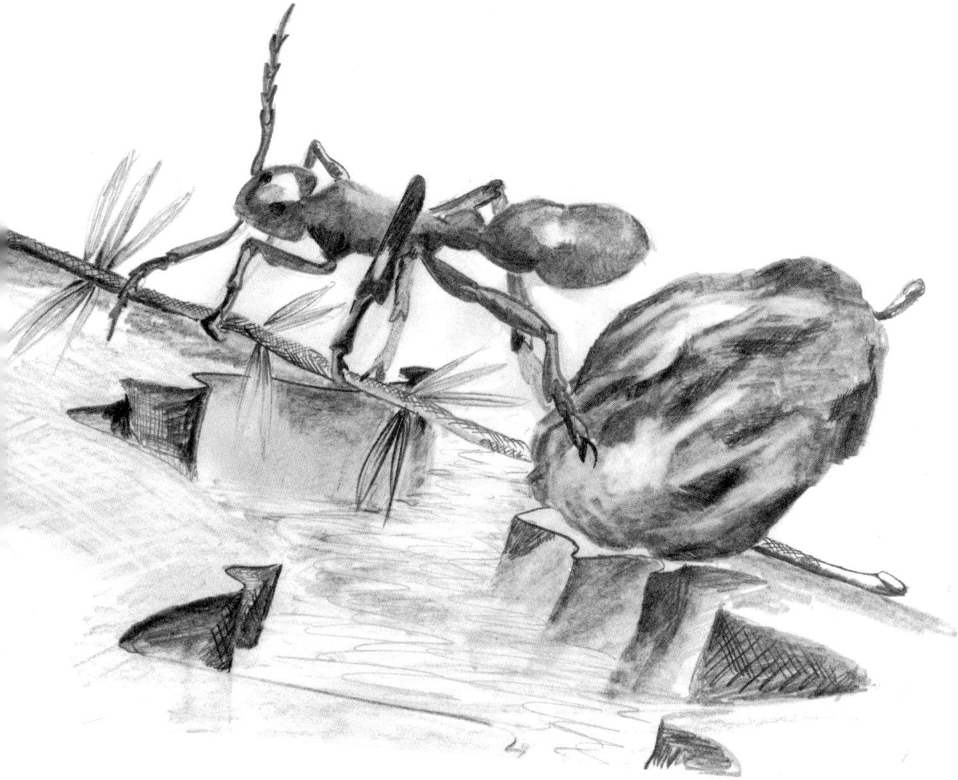

Type 1

right into the middle of the road. At the same time she hurried to get to the head of the column so that she could supervise the unloading and stacking process. Round the next bend in the road the ant-hill came in sight and Carla and her young workers marched towards the storage depot.

'Remember now,' said Carla, 'remember that the goods must be stored separately. Raisins here, fruit over there and crumbs towards the front.' And with one feeler she pointed in the right direction, while the other was raised in admonition. The best thing will be for you all to form a row and...'

But she had hardly finished speaking before the young ants were running here and there in all directions to the store-rooms.

'Oh, why can't you do this properly,' groaned Carla, waving her feelers so violently that she gave herself a headache. ' Now, all of you, *get into a row!*'

But everything was already stored and the day's lesson was ended. The young ants disappeared into the ant-hill to attend to their other duties.

Carla too still had things to do. Cleaning duties were another part of her job. Still upset, she went down into the ant-hill to clean out the nurseries

'Let's hope that you at least will turn out to be orderly, well-regulated ants,' she told the larvae, as they gazed at her wide-eyed, 'because otherwise I see no future for our colony!'

She began to clear away the mess, she cleaned every nook and cranny and went on working long after everything was clean. Until late at night Carla was busy. At last she collapsed from sheer exhaustion and fell asleep on the spot.

And that was how the queen ant found her. The queen ant was a wise ruler. She told Carla to take a day off. Carla was

Type 1

very reluctant to comply, but she could not contradict the queen ant. That too was part of order in the colony.

So the next day saw Carla sitting in the grass among the fragrant flowers having a day off. She didn't work and she didn't bustle about anxiously, because she was an obedient subject and she submitted to the dictates of the queen, even when it was almost beyond her power to do so—as it was now.

Nevertheless, she managed to persevere all day, in accordance with order, and to sit still among the flowers—which was the proper way to spend a day off. Only now and then there was a twitching in her legs and in her feelers.

Type 1

(ii)
Let Your Wings Carry You

MANDALA the Bee sat at the flight-hole of her beehive grooming herself.

She was an exemplary bee, and so of course she groomed herself in exactly the order her mother had shown her: first the large left wing, then the large right wing, after that the small left wing and then the small right wing. Finally she brushed herself over the back legs, her whole body and the rest of her legs. With the right hind leg she cleaned the two right forelegs, with the left hind leg the two left forelegs. Finally the left hind leg brushed the right, and the right hind leg brushed the left, so that it looked as if both legs were hopelessly entangled.

But Mandala was not only exemplary, she was also neat and clever—and neat, clever bees never get their legs into a knot.

Behind the hills enclosing the great meadow the sun was rising. Soon it would be time to fly out to collect pollen. Mandala was one of those who would fly today for the first time.

This was a new sphere of work for her. She had already taken part in the various activities of the beehive, and so far had completed all her tasks with such great care that the other workers declared her a perfect bee. Of course Mandala was always glad when she heard them say that but it didn't make her complacent, for *she* didn't think herself perfect. And that was a shame, for there was actually nothing she longed

Type 1

for so much. 'Maybe,' she thought, 'maybe all I still need to make me perfect is to prove myself at food-collecting.' And as one after another the collectors left the beehive, Mandala spread her wings and flew with them.

It was a beautiful summer day. The sun shed its warm rays and flowers of all colours were everywhere in bloom. But Mandala noticed neither the sun nor its warmth. Her concern was with the flowers and only with those flowers whose colour promised a good harvest. She scanned the meadow beneath her.

It was an unwritten law that no bee might leave the meadow. It had never occurred to any worker to question this order, because to stay in the meadow was only reasonable. Everyone could see that no flowers grew on the hills around it and so there was nothing useful to be done there.

Far beneath Mandala gleamed a whole field of dandelions. Mandala stopped in mid-flight and alighted on the finest one of all.

'I do hope I'll get this right too,' she thought as she began to crawl in and out of the petals, getting the pollen stuck all over her fur until at last she looked as if she had been rolled in powder. But a quick glance at the neighbouring dandelions showed her that all the bees were doing exactly the same.

Flying off again Mandala used her hind-legs to brush the pollen from her body into the sac on her legs. In this way the pollen was compressed into a tight little orange ball.

'It could be rounder than that,' Mandala considered, with a critical glance behind her. And so after visiting the next flower she took pains to smooth out the unevenness.

So busy was Mandala with her work that she never noticed she was being followed from flower to flower by a gloriously shimmering butterfly. Only when he got directly in her way,

Type 1

almost turning her upside down, did she become aware of him.

'Hello sweetie,' said the butterfly.

'H'm, just what I could do without,' muttered Mandala, pretending she hadn't heard. Busily she went on running hither and thither.

'What's that you're doing?' asked the butterfly curiously, coming nearer and meanwhile coiling and uncoiling his long proboscis in a way which Mandala found very distasteful.

'You're confusing me,' she announced and retreated so close to the very edge of the flower that she almost fell out of it.

'Oh, so sorry,' said the butterfly. 'By the way, just call me James.' And he bowed with a charming flutter of his wings.

'How d'you do. My name is Mandala. Sorry, but I must ask you to excuse me now. I have a lot to get on with.' Buzzing loudly Mandala rose into the air and made a beeline for the next flower.

James the butterfly dipped his proboscis luxuriously into a drop of nectar and spread his wings in the sunshine. Then in a roundabout way and with a few little hops and skips he fluttered over to the flower where Mandala was hard at work, and settled there.

Somewhat annoyed, Mandala went on with her work. Meanwhile she was careful not to get too close to the butterfly who sat there in the middle of the flower opening and closing his wings. Mandala found it very tiresome to have him just sitting around and on the very spot, of all places, where she could have been collecting.

'Have you really got absolutely nothing to do?' she finally asked the butterfly in exasperation.

'Do call me James,' the butterfly reminded her as he stretched out comfortably in the sun. 'Aren't these flowers

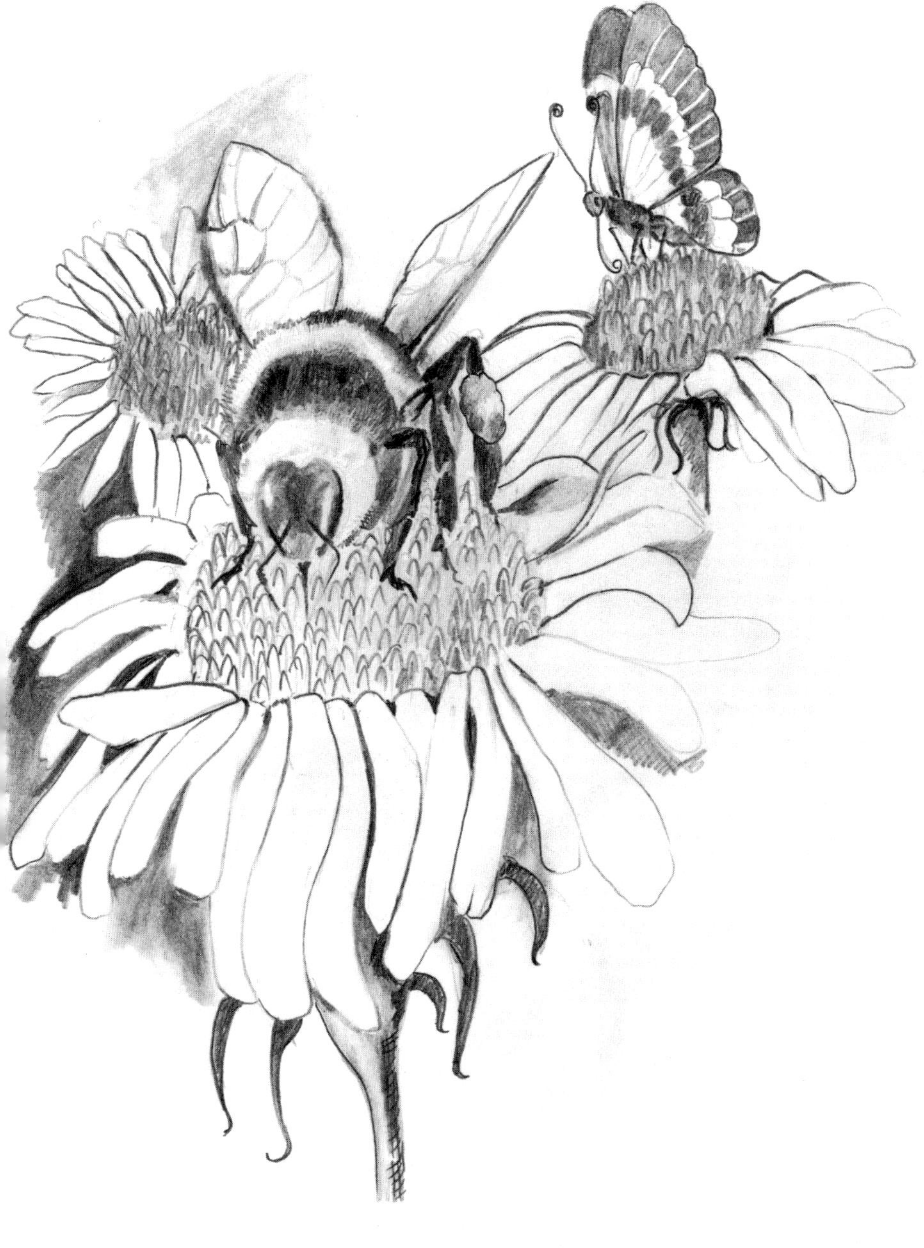

Type 1

wonderful? We do live in a perfect creation, don't we!'

Mandala felt her temper rising. This butterfly was getting on her nerves.

'In the first place, no, we do not live in a perfect creation—I happen to know that for a fact,' she buzzed vehemently, and it was only with a great effort that she managed to suppress her indignation, 'and secondly, I did ask you, what do you actually *do* all day long!'

'What do I do?' repeated James. 'I celebrate life!'

'I beg your pardon?' Mandala thought she couldn't have heard correctly. 'Celebrate life? Life is hard work, not celebration!'

By now thoroughly worked-up, she brushed the pollen from her fur and stuffed it into her sac. And in doing so she forgot, out of sheer agitation, to be careful to make the ball of pollen as round as possible.

James watched her for a while in bewilderment.

'You make life into hard work and that's why for you it's imperfect,' he said at last, 'and I make life a celebration and that's why it's perfect for me. It's as simple as that.'

And he turned to the next flower to refresh himself from an iridescent dewdrop.

Mandala looked across at him indignantly. How could he think like that—so irresponsibly. If everyone had that attitude, how would any work ever get done? One ought to keep clear of such people! All the same, she followed the butterfly after a while.

'Tell me, where do people learn that way of thinking, Mr...er...James?'

James touched her lightly with his long feelers, and Mandala started back. 'It's not something you learn. It just comes from inside,' he answered. 'I'm delighted to find you're interested. It will certainly do you good.'

Type 1

Before Mandala had a chance to protest, he went on: 'I'll help you. You'll see how easy it is and afterwards you'll feel much better. The best way to start is by becoming an esoteric—like me.'

'An *esoteric*? What's that?' asked Mandala, quite mystified.

'An esoteric is someone who lets his wings carry him,' replied James. 'You need a lot of practice in that.'

'Not at all,' retorted Mandala, 'I've known how to fly for ages.'

'I didn't say *use* your wings,' James corrected her, 'I said: let yourself be carried by them. There is a difference. Come with me, we'll try it out straight away!'

And he had already caught Mandala by the feeler and was flying away with her.

'But…' objected Mandala, 'I've still got…good gracious me, you're flying so high.'

'Don't stiffen up like that,' James told her, 'just let go…yes, that's it, that's better. Just for once forget about your work for a while and let yourself be carried!'

'Where to?' asked Mandala breathlessly.

'Everywhere! Or nowhere! Wherever you like,' cried the butterfly. 'Let the sunshine caress you, and open yourself to the joy of being loved by life!'

Mandala saw that they were just about to fly over the hills, and she shivered—but she couldn't quite tell whether it was with fear or joy.

James and Mandala flew over houses where people lived, over cows and horses peacefully grazing in the pastures; they flew over a little pond and saw themselves reflected in its water and they rocked to and fro on a buttercup.

When at last they returned to the meadow the sun was already setting.

Type 1

'James, that was the loveliest day of my life,' sighed Mandala as they landed. 'Thank you!'

'I've kept you from your collecting though, haven't I!' James reminded her.

'Oh, never mind,' laughed Mandala, 'I'll easily catch up with that tomorrow.'

With a gentle pressure of their feelers they parted and Mandala, humming with happiness, flew back to her beehive, where she deposited both her pollen-balls.

They were rather small and not at all round—but Mandala didn't mind about that in the least.

Type Two

(i)

Love Cannot Be Earned

SARA THE DONKEY was getting old and her coat was worn through to the hide with all the loads she had carried.

Every morning, well before sunrise, she set out with Caleb her master on the long and difficult trek over the hills to Jerusalem.

Every morning she carried two big baskets full of earthenware—one on her left side and one on her right—and for a week now she had been carrying Caleb as well. He walked along beside her as a rule, but just now he had an inflamed foot and found walking too difficult.

Sara knew very well that she was the sole support of Caleb and his family, because only she was able to carry Caleb's earthenware to market in Jerusalem.

Careful and steady, she put one hoof in front of the other so as not slip on the stony pebbles. One more bend in the road and there before her was the city wall of Jerusalem. They hadn't far to go now.

She took the last lap at a gentle, cautious trot, for the sooner they reached the market-place the better chance Caleb would have of finding a good place to display his wares.

Caleb stroked the donkey's neck. 'Dear old Sara. What would I do without you!'

A warm feeling of happiness and pride flowed through Sara. Life was wonderful and she was strong. Yes, the more Caleb needed her the stronger she was!

Type 2

Arriving at the market-place Caleb unloaded the baskets from Sara's back. She stood as close to him as she could so as to spare him exertion—and also, perhaps, to let him see how sore her back was where the baskets had rubbed against it. Then she trotted over to the other donkeys congregated at the edge of the market-place.

Now began the most useless part of Sara's day, when she had nothing to do. Real life would only resume in the evening when she would be loaded up again—this time of course with lighter baskets, but all the same...

That evening when Sara was back in her stall and Caleb had brought her fodder and given her a grateful stroke, Eli, her foal, came to her. Eli was a sturdy little donkey and already nearly as big as his mother. Soon he too would be able to carry baskets of earthenware to market.

Sara didn't care to think about that. At present *she* was Caleb's sole support and that was how she liked it. But what will a mother not do for her children! There comes a time when she even has to hand over to them the responsibility for taking care of her master. And when she does, not even then can she be sure that her child will be grateful to her ever after!

With a sigh Sara turned towards him. 'You are a great burden, my son,' she said, 'but I love you all the same.

Eli looked at his mother in astonishment. 'A burden? But you never carry *me*!'

Gently Sara nuzzled his short stubbly mane. 'Later on, when you have done as much for your children as I have, then you will understand what I mean.'

Eli looked thoughtfully into the distance. 'I've got a question, Mum,' he said at length.

'Ask it then,' Sara encouraged him. 'The best thing you can do with all your problems is to come straight to your mother for advice.'

Type 2

'Mum, what is it like carrying baskets day after day? Don't you ever wish you could do something different? What does it feel like only ever to *help* people?'

Sara gave a snort of disapproval. 'I once knew a black horse, my son, who always wanted to know what this or that *felt* like. A *proper* donkey doesn't ask questions like that.'

Eli gazed at her wide-eyed. 'Why not?'

'We donkeys are proud to be able to serve our masters— *that* is what life is all about,' answered Sara. 'All the other things are unimportant. And that's why we don't ask questions about them.'

'But to *me* they are important,' Eli insisted obstinately, and stamped his hoof. 'Only, I do wish I knew what other things there were, anyway!'

'There is nothing else, my son, that is of any importance for you,' said Sara and she licked Eli's face fondly. 'One day you will see that too. Humans value us for the help we give them. And because they are grateful to us, we are perfectly happy to go on helping them over and over again.'

Eli made a face as if he had toothache. 'But there must be something else you would like! Have you got no wishes at all?'

'But of course I have, my son,' replied Sara. 'My greatest wish is for you to be like me one day.'

Eli said nothing more after that and turned away to drink some water from his trough.

Sara, however, watched him anxiously. Somehow, her son had escaped her influence. It was now up to her to get Eli back on the right track.

Next morning Caleb did not go to market. His foot was worse and he could not get up.

'You will see,' Sara told Eli, after Caleb's wife had brought them fresh hay, 'you will see there'll be no stroking today. People love us only for the work they get out of us.'

15

Type 2

It looked as if she was right. It was afternoon before Caleb's wife came back—and then only to clean out the stall. Without saying a word she took both donkeys outside and tethered them at the front door of the house.

Out on the road Sarah broke into loud braying: 'Oh, what ingratitude! Day after day I have sacrificed myself, and now I'm treated as if I were thin air—ee-aw, ee-aw!'

A short way off two men were walking along the street They kept looking round on all sides as if in search of something. They brightened when they heard Sara braying and hurried towards her.

'This is an ass's foal all right,' said one of the men and proceeded to untie Eli's rope.

'Hadn't we better take the she-ass?' suggested his companion. 'She looks more impressive. Maybe she's the right one.'

'No,' replied the other. 'The Master said he wanted a colt.'

Caleb, who had heard this exchange in front of the house came hobbling to the window. 'Hey! What are you doing with my donkey?' he cried.

'The Master needs him,' said one of the men. We'll bring him back tonight.'

Caleb made no more objections and lay down again.

But Sara pricked her ears when she heard the word 'needs'. 'Mee-tooo, meeeee-toooooo,' she brayed. But the men were already on their way with Eli.

Just in time Sara remembered to bray some bits of advice after her son: 'If there are two baskets you must balance them out so the weight is the same right and left. And stand up straight—chest out, head up! And don't forget: you'll only be patted and stroked if you've been a real help!'

She couldn't advise him any more, as Caleb's wife came and led her back into the stall.

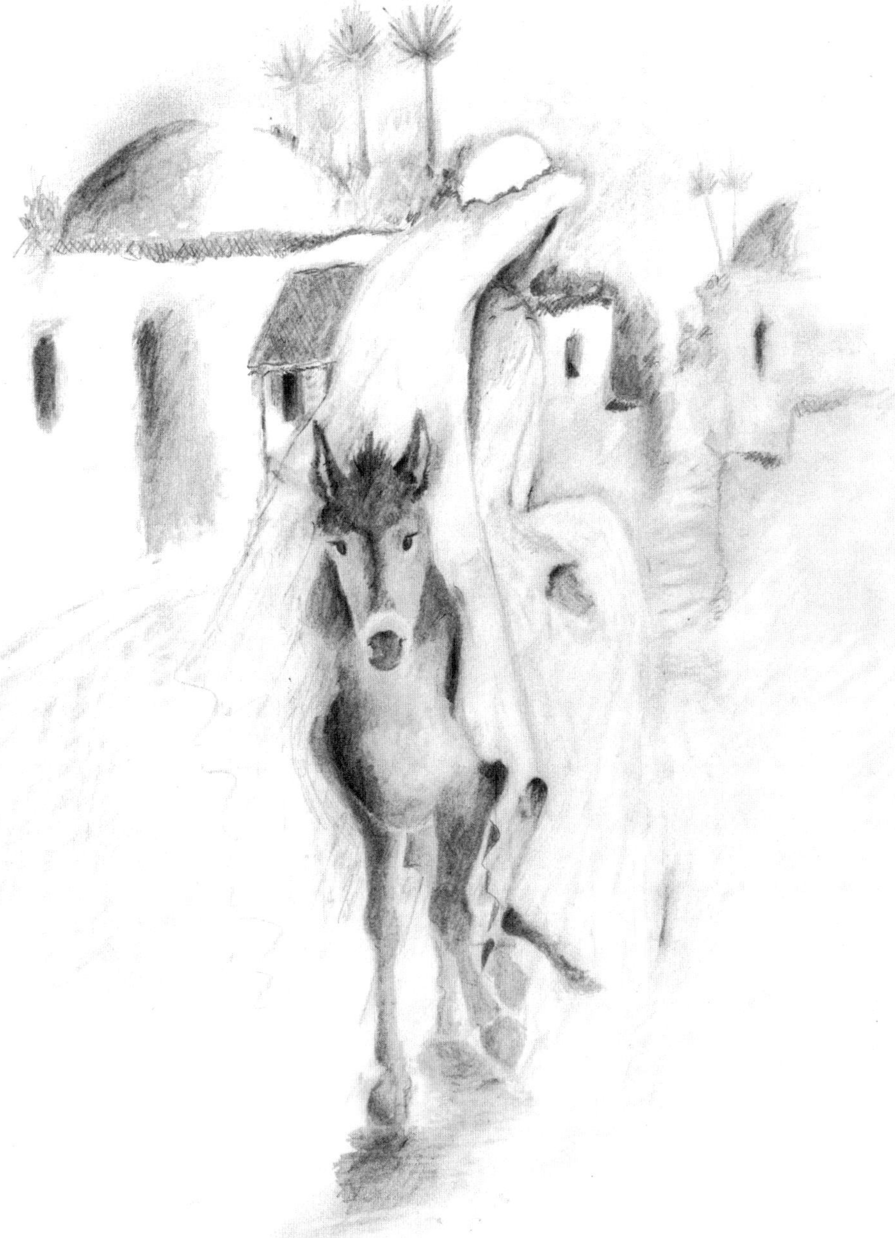

Type 2

Late that evening Eli was brought home.

'Well, my son,' asked Sara, when they were alone, 'how many loads did you have to carry? Did the Master pat you and stroke you afterwards? Come and tell me all about it. Now you've done something you can be really proud of!'

Eli looked at her and his eyes shone.

'The Master the men brought me to was a king. I didn't carry any load at all, but the king rode on me himself, just as if I was a noble horse. And do you know what? He looked at me and loved me, even before I'd done anything for him at all!

'And is that something I'm to be proud of? As if the Master needed me! Just the opposite: I needed him! Because he has shown me that real love can never be earned!'

Type 2

(ii)
It's a Thankless World

WITH TAIL erect, Mia the Cat picked her way daintily across the farmyard.

The farmyard was her home and here she was indispensable—in all sorts of ways: without Mia the trouble with mice in the barn would have got out of hand long ago; without Mia the three little kittens lying in a sheltered corner of the cowshed would have no mother; and without Mia the farmer's children would have no pet to stroke and cuddle. Without Mia the farmer's wife would have no idea what to do with her kitchen scraps; and not least, the animals who lived here needed her too—as an understanding and helpful friend.

It was just as well Mia was there. Mia could see that nothing on the farm would function properly without her. And so she made it her business to be continually going the rounds, making sure that everything about the place was running smoothly.

Mia was just on her way to her three kittens. They were the fruit of an ardent love-affair with a tom-cat, a blind cat, as it happened, but his disability had made no difference to Mia. On the contrary, she had been only too glad to help and support him and he too had been very grateful to her—at first. However he had been unworthy of her love. He had proved that not long ago, by simply leaving her—after all she had done for him.

Type 2

Mia stepped into the hiding-place in the cowshed where her three kittens were already mewing piteously for her. Fondly she licked the little creatures and let each of them have a drink. It was not the poor children's fault, after all, that their father had treated Mia so badly. Mia stayed for a long time with her kittens, warmed them and fed them, and enjoyed the feeling of being such a good, kind mother .

Not until each kitten in turn was fully satisfied and had let go of her and fallen asleep did she allow herself to get up and have something to eat. A mouse would do.

It was about time to resume her work in the barn. For several days she had not had much opportunity for catching mice, and on no account could she disappoint the farmer. Mia knew how greatly he valued her services—that was the foundation of their relationship which on her side meant a great deal to Mia too.

She loved to feel his powerful hands stroking her and she liked the smell of tobacco in his clothes when she lay curled up purring in his lap or rubbed herself against his trouser legs.

But it cost her a pang sometimes to see that the farm dog also enjoyed the farmer's affection. She was never quite sure which of them the farmer loved more. One thing was certain, though: nobody loved the farmer more than *she* did.

To get to the barn on the opposite side of the farmyard Mia went round the dung-heap and, purring benevolently, slipped past the hens and rabbits.

Hens and rabbits were stupid. But Mia didn't look down on them, she would help even stupid creatures any time if they were in need. All the animals who lived here needed help. Except herself.

She had never appealed for help to anyone. To whom could she appeal anyway? There simply was nobody on this farm who could ever give her what she gave to others.

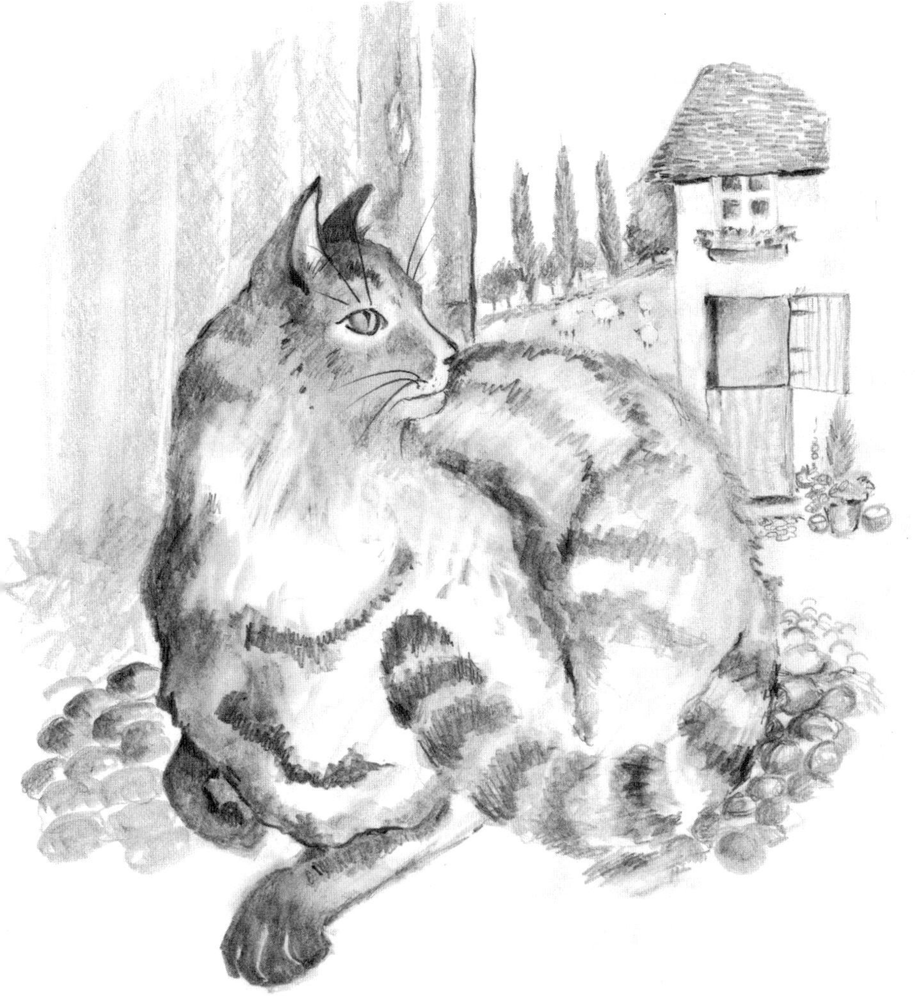

Type 2

In the space of the few days during which Mia had been fully occupied with her maternal duties, the mice in the barn had multiplied by leaps and bounds. Mia did her best to catch as many of them as possible. There were far more than she could ever eat.

To let the farmer see later on what she had achieved Mia arranged her catch, neatly stacked, in a heap at the door.

The work was strenuous and by the time Mia had cleared the barn of mice she was ready to drop. All she needed now was someone or other to come to her looking for help with their little problems! But today she simply didn't want to know. She was finished!

Wearily she trailed across from the barn to the farmhouse, to console herself with a bit of sweet cream and let the farmer's wife stroke her. It was the least she deserved.

She was just disappearing into the kitchen when around the corner came her best friend, the cat from the neighbouring farm. She wanted to talk to Mia and get her advice. 'But of course, my dear,' said Mia. 'You know I've always got time for you.'

It was late in the evening when Mia was at last able to slip into the farmhouse. By now not only was she utterly exhausted but she could have bitten off her tail for letting everyone make use of her.

But when she entered the living-room and saw from the farmer's beaming face that he was pleased with her (he must already have seen the heap of mice in the barn) she allowed the children to pet her for a bit. Only after that did she make her way back to her saucer in the kitchen.

And there a shock awaited her: sitting under the kitchen table, in a little basket lined with covers, was another cat! She was still very young and, to human eyes, extremely sweet. At once Mia hated her with all her heart.

Type 2

For years she, Mia, had been catching the mice on this farm all by herself, she had played with the children, and had always fulfilled her other tasks to the farmer's entire satisfaction. She had sacrificed herself to the needs of all the other animals on the farm and in recent weeks had even neglected her own kittens in order to carry out her duties. And now another cat, a complete and utter stranger, had been brought into the house!

Clearly she was being given to understand that she was no longer needed. Evidently she didn't catch mice quickly enough for the farmer, and yet just now he had seemed to be looking at her with approval. Or was she no longer pretty enough for the children? Yes, that was probably it!

She was quite aware that she was getting on and had for a long time looked less appealing than a young cat. But did they have to let her know it in such a mean way? Was this all the thanks she was to get for her services? That farmer didn't deserve to have one more mouse caught for him. If she was no longer wanted here, very well, she would go!

The farmer and his family never saw Mia again. She disappeared for good, together with her children. No one guessed that it had anything to do with the little cat who, a short while afterwards, was collected by her owners on their return from holiday.

The farmer's family had only been looking after her.

Type Three

(i)

Who Am I Without My Colours?

CHARLIE MELEON sat on a branch high up in the tallest tree of the forest, busily diffusing a yellow glow. That was nothing unusual for him. Charlie's repertoire included a whole range of different colours, but when he wanted to be seen, the most appropriate colour seemed to be yellow.

And he did want to be seen. Because after all, he had managed to climb higher up this tree than any other chameleon before him. It had taken him half the afternoon to do it, and before sunset he would have reached the top—he was quite certain on that point.

Visible for miles around, he went on getting yellower and yellower, at the same time rotating his eyes in various directions in order to test reactions to his activities. It was reassuring to find that he had been seen and that the forest animals were looking up at him in admiration.

That really would have been enough to satisfy him. But he also wanted to know if he could be recognised from the air or whether in fact the branches of the tree were hiding him from view; and so he rolled his eyes upwards.

And there he saw something which in more senses than one brought him up short. Above him a big furry animal was hanging upside-down from a branch—a branch that was higher than the one on which he, Charlie, was sitting. That was one thing. Another thing was that it didn't seem to occur to this animal to look at him.

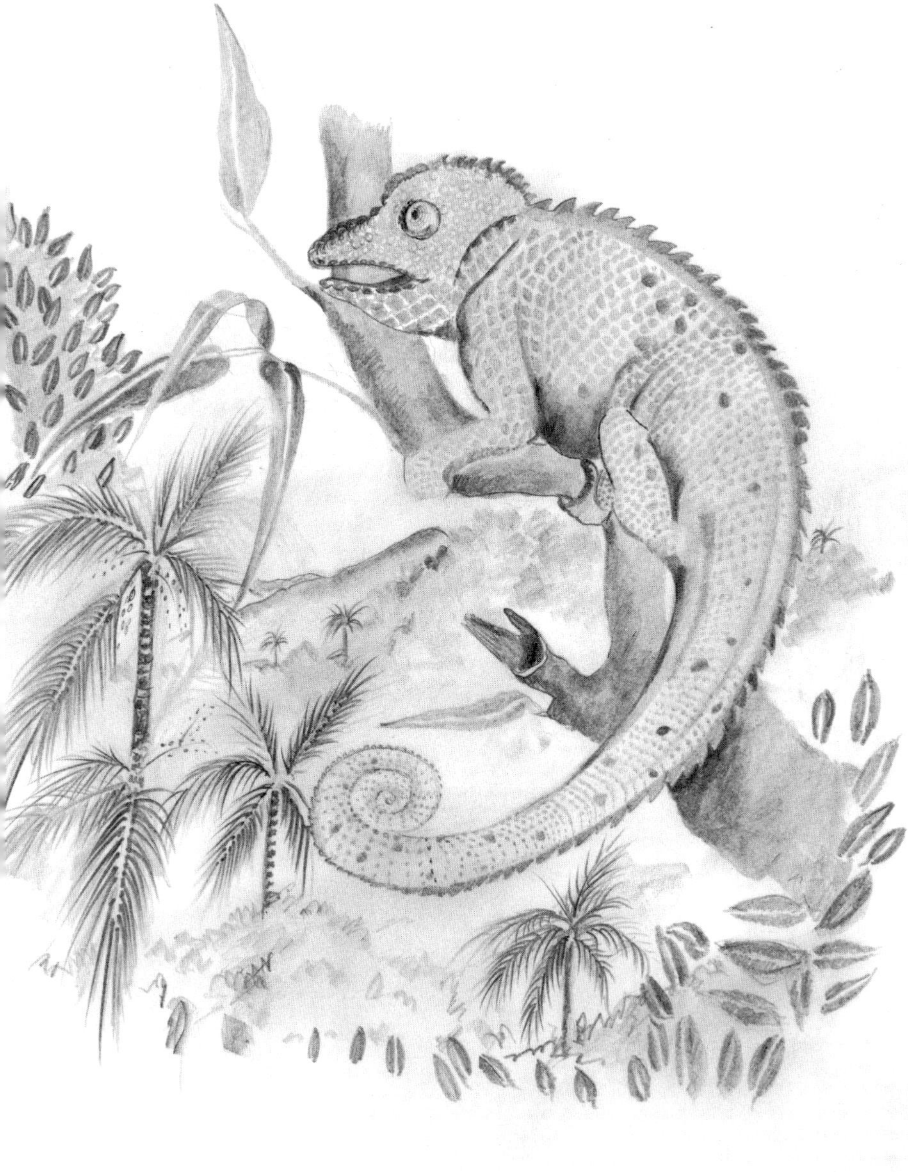

Type 3

Well, that couldn't seriously bother Charlie Meleon. He was after all the kind of guy that couldn't care less whether other animals noticed him or not.

To make this clear to all the ones below who continued to gaze up at him the whole time, Charlie changed his colour to a cool, understated blue-green.

Relaxed and unconcerned, he snapped up with an elegant flick of his tongue a fly that was just sneaking past him, and chewed it calmly.

And then, without any hurry, he resumed his climb to the top. He went on climbing until he had found a branch from which he could look down at the strange animal. There he settled and nonchalantly surveyed the scene below.

After some time the animal began laboriously to open one eye. With this he looked at Charlie, expressionless, while the other eye remained shut.

'Hi,' said Charlie, and switched to a dynamic red. 'I'm on my way to the top of the tree. I'm here on a business trip, okay? I've got the job of measuring this tree. I guess it's the tallest in this forest—right?'

It was impossible to tell from the eye if the animal had grasped the meaning of these words.

Charlie's red became somewhat more intense. 'It's taken me ten minutes to get to this height from the ground. Pretty good, huh? How long did it take you to get up here?'

The only reaction from the animal was that the eye closed again just as slowly as it had opened.

'Ya won't get an answer from him so fast' said a voice behind Charlie, 'don't ya know that's the sloth?'

Charlie turned round. Behind him was a monkey dangling from a branch and swinging to and fro. With one hand he held on and with the other he scratched himself extensively. He gave Charlie a friendly grin and Charlie grinned back.

Type 3

'I wasn't expecting any answer from the sloth,' he rejoined. Besides, I guess it'll be more entertaining talking to you!'

As he spoke lots of different-coloured spots appeared on his red skin and gradually merged together.

'Fun, isn't it, doing somersaults in the trees at this height. I sure love climbing for a living.'

'Fun! Yeah!' giggled the monkey, swinging himself on to Charlie's branch and prancing about on it. 'I like fun!'

'D'you know this one?' asked Charlie and told the joke which always went down well with these types.

The monkey laughed so much that he almost fell off the branch and then immediately cracked a few jokes of his own.

Then Charlie told him all the hilarious things that had happened to him that day, and the monkey laughed and Charlie's colours became more and more vivid.

'You are boring me. Let me sleep,' a voice drawled underneath them

Charlie bent down and observed that the sloth had now got both eyes half open.

'Well, what d' ya know—woken up, have you?' he cried jovially, and brought off the feat of turning red on the side facing the sloth while his other side remained spotted.

The sloth, from under his heavy lids, looked past him and said nothing.

'I got up this tree in three minutes. How about that, huh? Everyone I've met tells me they've never done it so fast. What do you think, buddy?,' he asked, turning to the monkey. But the monkey had already gone.

'Changing your colours like that, it's pointless, utterly pointless,' said the sloth sleepily, while he contemplated the different-coloured halves of Charlie's body with glazed eyes.

This observation was so unexpected and so direct that Charlie had to struggle briefly with a rising sense of insecurity before he got himself back under control.

Type 3

He was just about to make some sarcastic reply when the sloth began to speak again: 'Much better to sleep, then you don't waste all that energy. It's all the same, you know. Why make an effort? The world is coming to an end anyway...just as you are...why wear yourself out? It's all the same in the end...so it might as well come...to an end...now...'

The sloth spoke more and more slowly. Obviously it had not said so much for a very long time. Now it heaved a deep sigh and draped itself in slow motion in a more comfortable position.

'...then you'll have gotten it over with at least,' it mumbled thickly by way of conclusion and again it sank back into its previous trance-like state.

Charlie's colours had paled. While the sloth was speaking he had felt he was being drawn slowly and relentlessly into a bottomless pit. Everything pointless—everything in vain... Charlie sensed that none of his colours could get him out of this one. And even if they could...he was suddenly...no longer capable of producing any colour at all!

When he realised this, he felt paralysed. His head swam, he lost his grip and before he knew what was happening he had fallen off his branch.

The first thing Charlie was aware of when he came to was that he was lying on the ground, in the dusk, among the bushes and undergrowth. There was no living creature to be seen anywhere. He was alone.

The next thing he noticed was far worse: he no longer had any colour! His skin was exactly the same shade of grey as the twilight all around him.

Charlie was seized with panic. Who was he then, without his colours? Was he anybody at all? No, he was NOTHING!

This knowledge shot through him like lightning. And in the same moment he saw clearly that there were two

Type 3

possibilities before him: either he would have to look this fact in the face and accept himself as he was—or get up the nearest tree and start putting on the act again.

Like a shot Charlie was on his feet and running for all he was worth. Away! just get away from here.

A few yards off he could see a flock of parrots perched on a tree. As Charlie dashed towards them he recovered his orientation, and knew what personality he could assume next: flamboyant, swaggering, 'The Great I Am'.

He was somebody again.

Type 3

(ii)
The True Self Is Behind the Facade

THE FIRST Conference for Self-Discovery was to be held in a big meadow in the middle of the aviary. The organiser and public relations manager of this event was Victor the Peacock.

He had planned and organised the whole thing down to the smallest detail, and weeks in advance had set up an ambitious advertising campaign which had attracted the attention not only of the inmates of the aviary but also of many other creatures in the surrounding area. The theme of the conference, expressed in crisp contemporary idiom was : 'Who Am I Really? The Way to the True Centre'.

At last the day of the Conference arrived. Victor had been very busy since early morning putting the finishing touches to the programme until it positively shone with perfection.

His own appearance too was thoroughly spruced up. After all it was he, Victor, who had to present the programme effectively. For Victor was not only Organiser and PR Manager, he was also President and Principal Speaker at the Conference. Victor preened himself and arranged each feather individually. And finally he got his wife, a quite ordinary and unpretentious hen, to inspect his supporting quills. These quills were important because they helped to fan out his magnificent wheel and if they were not sitting correctly his tail feathers did not stand up half so impressively. Not until he was satisfied that his appearance was faultless did Victor set out for the meadow

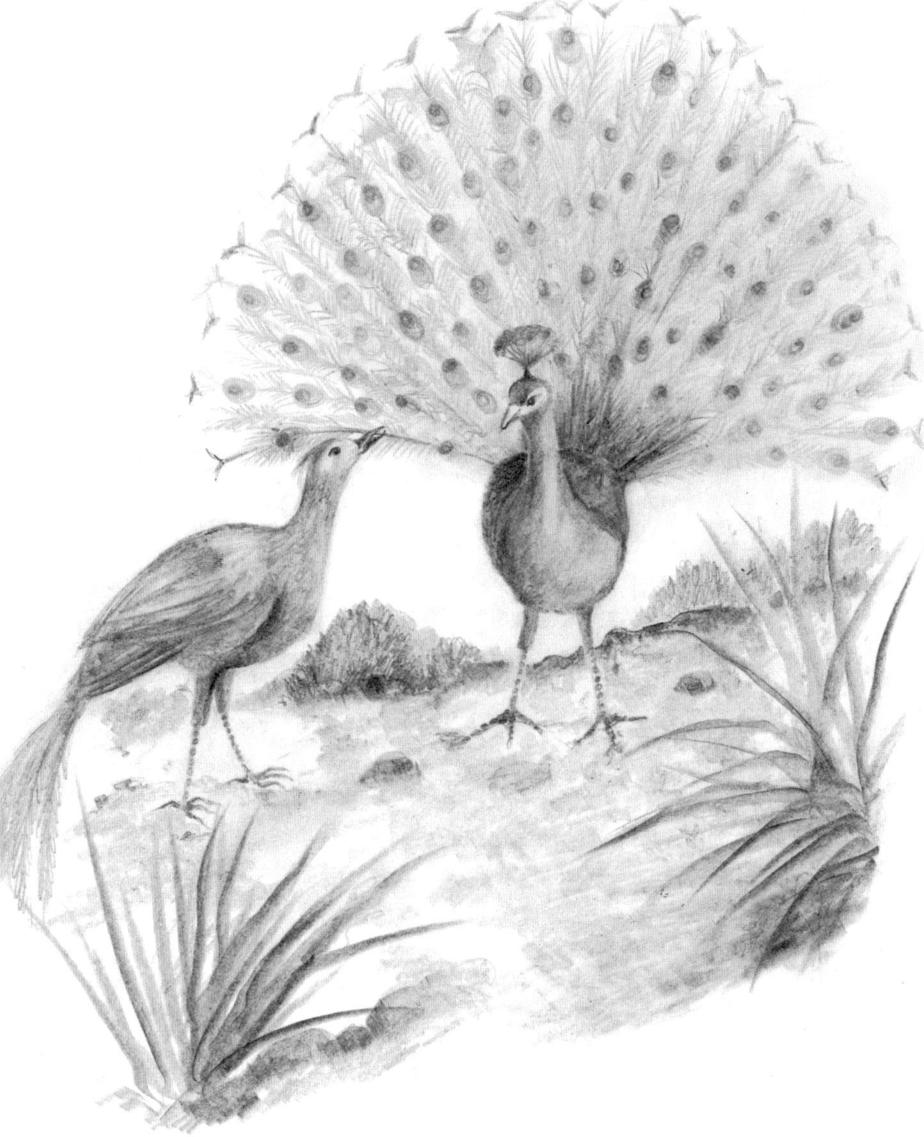

Type 3

The assembly-ground was already swarming with visitors. The majority were inhabitants of the aviary—owls, partridges, wild geese and ducks—but also some of the four-legged animals of the neighbourhood. All were chattering, squawking and crowing at the same time.

Victor waited until the excitement had died down a little, then he stepped onto the platform. It was a brilliant entrance. By the end of his first three sentences Victor had the audience completely spell-bound. And after another three sentences there was not one member of the audience who was not fully convinced that what he needed more than anything else was the very thing that Victor was extolling: true self-knowledge.

'So what it means, my friends,' said the peacock, bringing his brilliant speech to a close and emphasising the meaning of his words with an equally brilliant display of tail feathers, 'what it means is that we have to learn to live as we really are—without masks and pretences. And that is what we are going to work at together. Thank you for your attention.'

Victor acknowledged the deafening applause that now broke out with a bow that was meant to look modest. He then went on, with a few pithy words, to open the meeting for discussion.

It was some time before one of the participants ventured to speak. It was the owl. She stood up and cleared her throat.

'In principle I share the speaker's concern for spiritual development,' she said cautiously. 'But I would just like to observe that self-knowledge is in the first place something that each of us must find for ourselves, in our own depths, and in solitude.'

'Thank you so much for that contribution,' said Victor quickly. 'Now would anyone else care to take up another point?' And as he spoke he looked round in a casual sort of way for the eagle, whom he had hoped would have something to say; but the eagle was not present.

Type 3

'If there are no more questions,' continued Victor,' we can come straight to the real object of this meeting. I intend to set up a workshop for self-discovery. A workshop in which we shall be able to learn together and share our experiences. An objective of this kind suggests the possibility of founding an Association to give the whole project an appropriate form.'

This idea met with general approval and on the very same day the 'Association for Self-Discovery' was brought to birth. Victor was unanimously elected Chairman, Vice-Chairman, Treasurer and Secretary.

The Association proved to be a complete success and Victor was very satisfied—until one day he became aware of alarming physical symptoms. First of all his supporting quills ceased to function properly and he could no longer hold his tail feathers erect in a wheel—to his great embarrassment and to the detriment of his image. For the time being however, Victor was clever enough to conceal it.

Then one day something even worse happened. The tail feathers themselves began to loosen. It looked as if at some point they were going to fall out!

Victor now began seriously to dread an imminent loss of prestige and so he decided to suspend his work for the time being and stay at home until he was fit to be seen again.

'Good idea,' his wife encouraged him. 'After all, the work doesn't really amount to very much, does it? Or have you already found yourself meantime ?'

That was a very frank and direct question, but Victor preferred not to answer it. Spreading his feathers he began to talk about training programmes and effective meditation exercises, quoting statistics which showed that membership of the Association was rising steeply and its funds were on the increase

But that wasn't at all what Victor's wife wanted to hear. 'Unless you find *yourself* in your Association for Self-

Type 3

Discovery,' she maintained, 'everything you're doing is pure shadow-boxing in my opinion.'

That was a palpable hit.

Normally such words would have left Victor unmoved. But now, with drooping tail-feathers on the point of falling out, he was really shaken.

And when a few days later his feathers actually did start to fall out it was like a further confirmation of what was happening inside. Everything in him was going to pieces. Suddenly his dazzling facade crumbled, the self-image he habitually presented to others faded away—and what was left?

Yes, indeed, what was left? For the first time in his life Victor was panic-stricken at the thought that there would be nothing left of him at all.

Then one night he had a dream. He dreamt he met the eagle, and asked him why he had not been at the conference. But instead of answering, the eagle just said, 'Come with me, I want to show you something!'

In the dream Victor could suddenly fly and the eagle took him up a high mountain, to a lonely mountain lake. The sun was shining, its rays reflected in the crystal-clear water; and Victor could see through it to the very depths.

Overwhelmed, he asked, 'Where am I?'

'You are in yourself,' replied the eagle. 'That's what you can be like, if you'll only stop deluding yourself.'

Then Victor woke up and for the first time he had fresh hope. If what he had seen in the dream was really inside him, then he no longer need worry about his image. He could even try to discover himself!

Type Four

(i)

All Animals Are Part of One Great Unity

THE HORSES who spent the day all together in the paddock already knew each other well, for they were brought there every morning. Most of the time they stood around in groups, grazing or playing. Only one horse always held aloof. That was Prince.

Prince was an exceedingly beautiful black stallion. He had a smooth gleaming coat, which shimmered almost blue in the sun, and he wore his long silky mane tossed carelessly to the left. His slender ankles were a mark of breeding, the powerful movements of his body indicated temperament; and his great expressive eyes gazed dreamily and often indeed, sadly, into the world.

Prince was a horse who drew all eyes. And when he cantered across the paddock with his splendid mane streaming in the wind, all the mares watched him in admiration.

But on this particular morning Prince didn't feel like galloping and letting his mane stream in the wind. Quiet and withdrawn, he stood in his favourite spot under the great weeping-willow and indulged his feelings. Deep within himself he was aware of an infinite sadness—a sadness which, as he vaguely perceived, had something to do with the fact that he was a stranger in this world...different from everyone else.

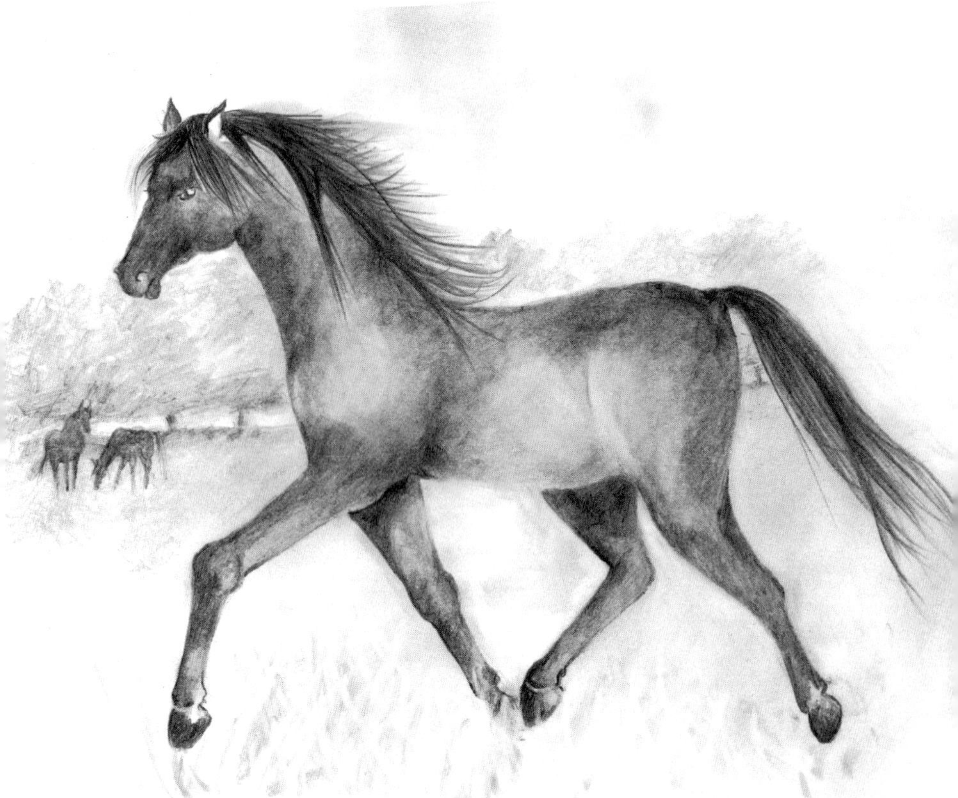

Type 4

He didn't know where this sudden sadness had come from until all at once he recalled his dream of the night before...

In the dream Prince had seen himself standing in a meadow. The grass looked green and lush, and Prince bent his head to eat it. But no sooner had he got a clump of grass in his mouth than a whole chunk of the meadow came out of the ground as well, with long roots dangling from it. Prince tugged and tugged and did not stop until he had torn all the roots out of the earth—and suddenly the grass was yellow and withered.

That was the end of the dream and Prince had woken up with the feeling that it was he who had been pulled up by the roots. Cut off from the source of life, uprooted, alone, and near to death, he was withering away...and no one noticed.

That was perhaps the worst of all. If he must suffer, why did he have to suffer without the others taking any notice? And the thought of that weighed him down with sadness more heavily than ever.

The great weeping-willow was shedding its red and brown leaves, for it was autumn. Prince found that very fitting. Nature too was dying. But nature was dying with style, clothed in appropriate shades of colour. He would like to do the same, to give artistic expression to his withering away.

Prince began to tug at the grass with his teeth. Not to eat it—no, that was for ordinary horses to do. For him it was now a creative act, a Happening. Each tussock that he pulled out of the earth made the same sound that he had distinctly heard in his dream, the sound of tender roots tearing and breaking.

And with every tussock he tore out, the infinitely mournful feeling of being uprooted grew stronger in Prince. Never before had these emotions been so profoundly interpreted in a creative act.

Type 4

It was only a pity that the other horses were standing too far off to be able to share in this experience. But it was part of the tragic life of an artist that his activities went unheeded. In any case he could not leave his place under the weeping-willow. The falling of withered leaves was all part of the artistic ambience of this Happening, and the only suitable framework for it. If the others didn't come to share in what he was doing, that only showed that they had very little understanding of art. Prince had the impression that none of the other horses had ever understood his artistic statements.

Suddenly he reared, and stopped what he was doing, with a horrid feeling that there was something alive in his mouth. Quickly he let go of the thing he had between his teeth: it was a plant with a bee crawling on it.

'Can't you watch where you're feeding?' buzzed the bee, very annoyed, and it flew aggressively to and fro in front of Prince.

Prince shied and retreated several steps. He had in the past had unpleasant experiences with these insects. They could jolt you painfully out of the loveliest dreams—as this one had just done. The beautiful, melancholy mood he had been enjoying was gone.

'I wasn't feeding,' protested Prince, 'I was expressing my feelings. You have spoilt the whole atmosphere. And atmosphere is the most important thing about a Happening.'

'What's a Happening?' asked the bee.

'The work of art that was being created here before you ruined it all was a Happening,' answered Prince.

The bee looked round and saw the torn-up clumps of grass. 'What's all this nonsense?' she muttered. 'You're not going to tell me that this is art!'

'You don't understand,' said Prince, and his voice had a very plaintive note. 'You can't ever have had the feeling of being uprooted and no longer one with Nature.'

Type 4

The bee thought this over for a while. 'Yes, I do know the feeling,' she replied. 'It's the feeling that somehow or other one isn't really as one ought to be...and it makes one feel very imperfect. But if *that's* your problem this is no way to solve it, you know, pulling up the grass like that. You've got to do something about it.'

'What I was doing with the grass wasn't trying to solve a problem, it was a profound artistic expression of my emotions,' explained Prince in aggrieved tones. 'You simply don't understand me.'

The bee looked at him attentively. 'True, I don't understand your art,' she said, 'but I think I understand your problem. If you'll take a tip from me: just forget about your art for once and enjoy all the things that are still perfect—this meadow for example. It's not right for you to tear the grass out by the roots just because *you* feel uprooted. And above all, don't just moon around! Find something to do! Now excuse me, I have work to get on with.'

With these words the bee flew away. Prince gazed mournfully after her. Of course he had always known it: nobody understood him. He bent down to resume his artistic occupation—but it didn't work the same as before. The beautiful, sad mood was ruined.

And instead of pulling up plants as he had intended, he simply looked at them. They really were perfect, just as the bee had said. The leaves were symmetrically arranged according to a definite pattern, and on the long stems sat the seeds which had formed from the blossoms.

Prince gently nudged one of them and at once the seeds were released from the plant in little parachutes and were carried away by the wind. Somewhere or other they would descend again and cause new plants to come to life. It was true what the bee had told him. It wasn't right just to uproot a plant like that.

Type 4

    Thoughtfully Prince began to eat—like all the other horses in the paddock. Gradually he moved away from his regular spot under the weeping-willow. With each step he took, countless numbers of these little parachutes flew up out of the grass in front of him and were whirled away.

    As Prince looked after them and reflected that it was he who had sent these seeds on their journey, something strange happened. All at once he realized that he—like the other horses and like all the other animals too—was only a small part of one great unity.

    And within this unity there was no dying for him to grieve over. There was only life—life and beauty forever renewing themselves in an endless cycle of death and rebirth. The seeds became new plants, the tree would put forth new leaves in the Spring and he, Prince, was a horse out at pasture and was doing what horses at pasture always do: munching the grass, and sending countless little parachutes flying through the air. No more and no less.

    In high spirits Prince galloped across the paddock to the other horses. Not because he wanted to let his mane stream in the wind, but just because he was enjoying it. It was a long time since he had been so happy.

Type 4

(ii)
An Aesthetically Beautiful Death, At Least

HIGH UP in the roof of the old barn, far above the farmer's pigs and cows and even above the hay-loft, home of the mice, Irmela the Carrier-Pigeon lived in a dovecote along with many other pigeons. Irmela was a special pigeon. She was the only one in the whole dovecote who was black, not white.

Every morning the farmer opened a little door to let the pigeons out for a walk on the roof, or to fly over the fields and vineyards.

And when evening came he climbed up by a narrow ladder into the dovecote and whistled a distinctive tune until all the pigeons had come in. Then the farmer shut the little door, for there were foxes and cats in the neighbourhood who would have been glad to climb onto the roof of the barn for a tasty morsel of pigeon.

Today Irmela was sitting all alone on the roof of the barn. The other pigeons had set off for a round trip in preparation for the flying competition that had been arranged in the neighbouring village, and which the farmer wanted his pigeons to enter.

Irmela had no enthusiasm for that sort of competitive racing. She was a carrier-pigeon and what she wanted was one day to deliver a proper, important letter and not just fly around racing with other pigeons.

A love-letter, for example…Irmela heaved a deep sigh and tucked her black head under her right wing. Yes, it must be a

Type 4

love-letter, elegantly written on the finest paper—scented if possible with rose or lavender.

She would take the envelope, carefully sealed with a kiss, (still perhaps faintly tear-stained) gently in her beak and deliver it to the beloved who would be awaiting it with longing. Oh, how beautiful that would be!

Tears filled Irmela's eyes and she buried her head even further under her wing. Oh, she knew what it was like to be parted from the beloved! Wistfully she thought back to the time when she had fallen passionately in love with a good-looking young cock-pigeon. How they had billed and cooed when they were together! And how she had suffered when he had to leave! Irmela sniffed. She was married to him now and all those lovely feelings were gone for ever.

In the farmyard below, the farmer's small son was herding the cattle into their stalls. Cow-bells tinkled as the herd came plodding down the hillside. The boy ran along barefoot behind them flourishing his stick.

Irmela did not even look. What happened here day after day on the farm was without any variation. In the morning the cows went out to pasture, the cow-sheds were mucked out, the animals fed, the hens' eggs collected, the tractor went here, there and everywhere; late in the afternoon the cows came home to be milked, and that was that. Every day the same. Nothing special ever happened.

Secretly Irmela envied the people, the animals and the other pigeons on the farm because this was all they needed to keep them happy. They had found their niche in this monotonous existence and couldn't imagine anything different. Irmela felt it to be her own personal tragedy that she expected more from life.

She drew her head out from under her wing and briskly fluffed out her crushed feathers so that she looked almost like a normal, healthy, cheerful pigeon. Then she rearranged each

Type 4

of her feathers in turn and with great skill, giving them just the right degree of casualness—not too much and not too little.

She did this so scrupulously and with such a sense of style, that she failed to notice a huge black cat climbing up onto the roof of the barn. Powerful and lithe, he crept up on Irmela who was just about to give her pinions a final flick, when she felt his hot breath on the back of her neck.

Startled, she turned round and found herself staring straight into his enormous green, hungry eyes. Quick as lightning the cat laid his great paw on Irmela so that she couldn't fly away. Then he settled down, purring, to contemplate the little black pigeon in comfort. His tail swished elegantly from side to side and his black silky fur gleamed in the evening sunshine.

Irmela continued to gaze into his eyes. She felt the concentrated energy emanating from this animal, saw his whiskers quivering and felt his warmth. He was dangerous, certainly, but also beautiful and full of vital strength.

This is the special thing I have always been looking for, she thought, and her heart beat fast with excitement. This is the stuff of life! And even if it means death for me, then at least it will be an aesthetically beautiful death: black cat and black pigeon in the setting sun...

Just as she was about to utter a last plaintive coo, the flock of pigeons, returning at that moment from their training flight, whirred close over the cat's head, startling him so that he let go of Irmela. And with a second swoop the pigeons succeeded in driving him away.

A handsome white cock-pigeon landed beside Irmela and drew her fondly under his wing. 'There you are, another close shave, my little dreamer,' he said.

Irmela sobbed.

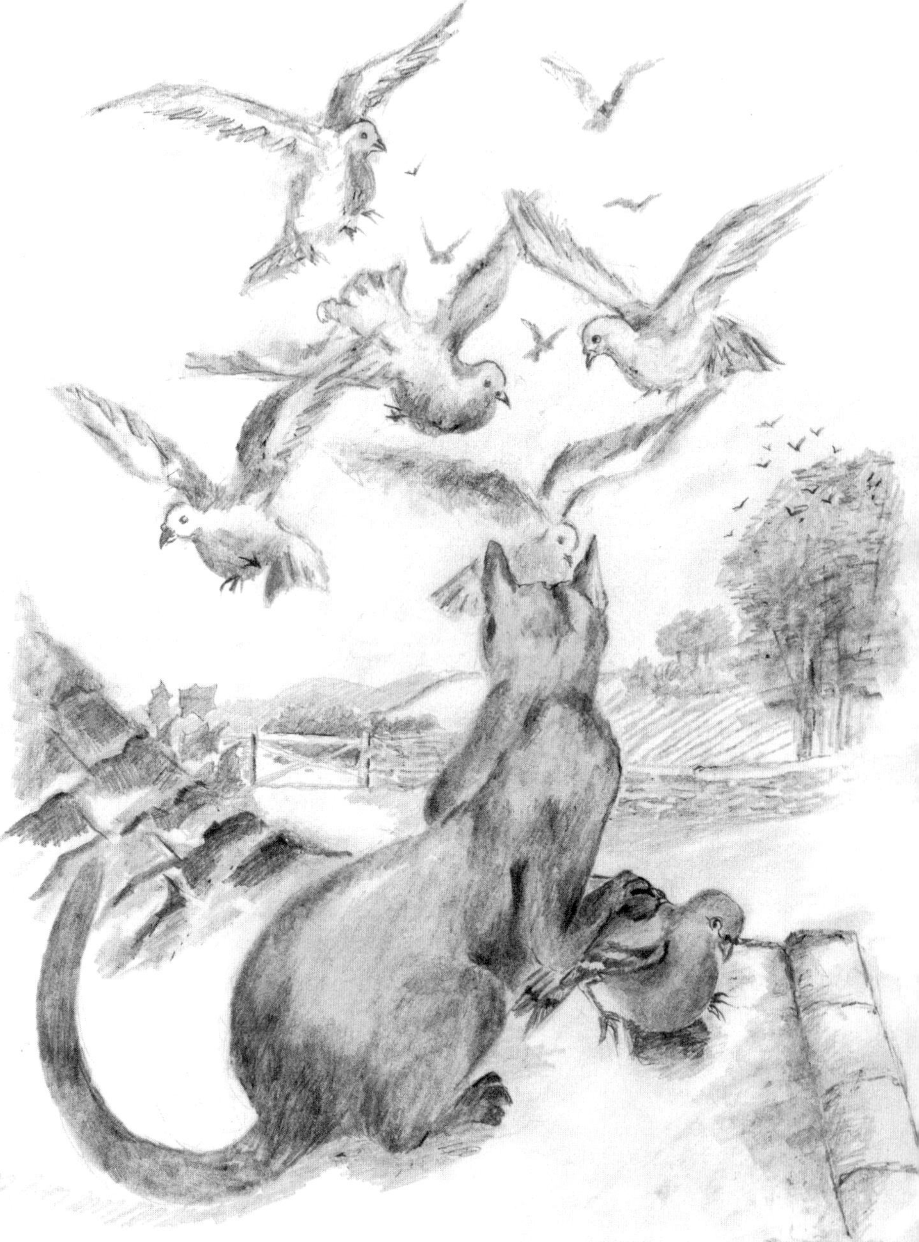

Type 4

'Don't cry, dear,' said another pigeon in motherly tones. 'It's the shock. It'll soon be over.'

And she put a comforting wing round Irmela's shoulders. But Irmela, with a vigorous movement, shook her off. 'Oh, none of you understands me,' she moaned.

And although the farmer had not yet begun to whistle, she flew through the little door into the dovecote, where she could brood in peace over that special feeling she had just had a moment ago.

Type Five

(i)

A Detached and Objective View of the World

IT WAS harvest-time in the wheat-field not only for the farmer but also for Paul Puffcheeks the Hamster.

Paul Puffcheeks was considered well-off, owing to the fact that his cheek-bags were always stuffed full. But he was also thought to be clever, and he had the reputation of being a somewhat eccentric intellectual—that was owing to his habit of sitting for hours on end in his house quite obviously doing nothing. In fact he spent this time ruminating on everything he had encountered outside.

The outcome of this was seldom very gratifying: he was continually being faced with the fact that all the animals round about were in a state of sentimental day-dreaming or emotional entanglement. Because that sort of thing was unfathomable and unpredictable, Paul Puffcheeks disliked it intensely. For him, even feelings of friendliness and partiality were suspect because he simply could not imagine their being genuine.

Paul Puffcheeks was a sceptic.

That is why he found it best to take as detached and objective a view of the world as possible—as indeed he did, and was evidently the only animal in the wheat-field to do so. It was just not given to everyone to have an intellectual grasp of life.

Paul Puffcheeks' residence—the only place on earth where he felt really comfortable—was large and spacious. It comprised several clearly separated and functionally-equipped

Type 5

rooms. But only one of these, the smallest, was where Paul actually lived and slept, for the hamster's wants were few. All the other rooms, which were arranged round the living-room from where they could be overlooked, served as storage space.

It always gave Paul Puffcheeks enormous satisfaction to lie in his bed-sitter and enjoy the sight of his full storage accommodation.

At present however his pleasure in this prospect was clouded. That was simply because in the last few days Paul had dug out more rooms and they were not yet filled—a state of things which of course could not be allowed to continue!

And so the hamster was pleased when one sunny autumn day he looked out of the entrance to his hollow and saw that the weather was just perfect for collecting.

Paul Puffcheeks loved collecting. It was one of the few activities which in his view could be really justified. He had no very high opinion of activity in general. As a matter of principle he held thought to be essentially superior to action.

Paul looked warily to right and left. He disliked company, especially when he was engaged in something as personal as collecting. And having first made sure there was no one anywhere near, he left his hollow. Nimbly he scampered from one ear of wheat to the next, stuffing the grains one by one into his cheek-bags. It would be a long time before they were full, for Paul's cheeks were incredibly elastic.

Finally he set out on a wider collecting expedition through the wheat-field. And as he collected, he pursued his own train of thought.

In his mind's eye the hamster could picture distinctly what the new store-rooms down below in his house would look like once they were filled with grains. It was a very pleasant picture and Paul was aware that even to think of those full

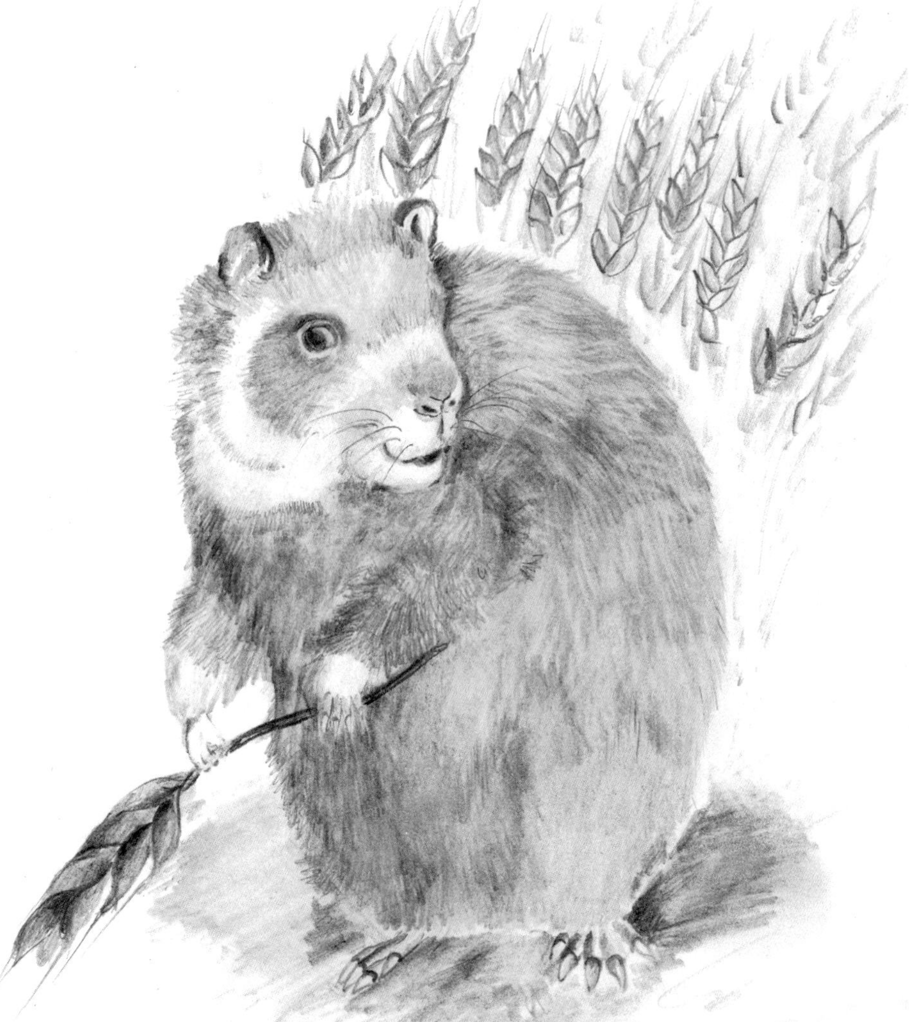

Type 5

store-rooms made him feel happy. The bare imagination meant more to him than the reality.

Actually, he thought to himself, he didn't need his store-rooms at all. Not, at any rate, for winter supplies. During his winter sleep he cut down his consumption to such an extent that almost all his stores were still intact when he woke up in the spring. He simply had no need of more. And one of the few things that he really enjoyed was managing to make do with as little as possible. But if he didn't need his store-rooms, what did he have them for?

It wasn't long before Paul got to the root of the matter: what they gave him was a comfortable feeling of repose and leisure—a feeling that was important in enabling him to recover from exhausting contacts with the other animals round about.

Paul Puffcheeks stuffed the last grains into his cheek-bags and set out on the way home, at the same time taking great care not to be seen by the other field-folk.

But he didn't manage to get back into his hollow unseen. When he was only halfway there he met a little lady hamster who, like himself, had been busy collecting. Unfortunately he noticed her too late to avoid her altogether.

'Oh, I *am* glad I've met you,' she cried, smoothing down her brown and white winter dress with a graceful movement. 'You see, I've got a bit of a problem! Could you relieve me of a few of my grains and carry them to my house? I'm afraid I've taken on rather more than I can cope with.'

And she giggled self-consciously, something which in a little lady hamster with cheek-bags stuffed to bursting is extremely attractive—to gentlemen hamsters at any rate.

Paul Puffcheeks did not answer at once. First of all he would have to think this over thoroughly before reacting, for it was full of imponderables.

Type 5

For one thing, feelings were involved here—that in itself was sufficient reason for reticence.

And then, what was being asked of him was to make contact, and what an intimate contact! To take grains out of her cheeks into his cheeks—good heavens above!

And perhaps this female hamster was trying to make up to him, and in fact had an eye on his stores. What she really wanted was to move into his comfortable winter quarters, and that would lead to his having to share everything with her—his grains and his cosy bed-sitter. There could be no question of it. And in any case, didn't he need all his stores for himself?

'Well, what about it? Are you going to help me or not?' demanded the lady hamster who had waited for Paul's answer long enough.

Oh, feelings again, this time quite different ones! Paul Puffcheeks was alarmed. The best thing would be to make off as quickly as possible. He mumbled something incomprehensible and pushed past her to get home fast.

But the lady hamster was not going to give up so soon, and she followed him.

Paul only wished he could vanish into thin air. But as he couldn't, he fixed his thoughts on a remote object so that the lady hamster, as far as he was concerned, simply wasn't there. He was an expert in this.

The little hamster went along beside him for a while, but seeing at last that Paul had inwardly withdrawn from her, she turned away in resignation.

Paul was relieved. He had a bit further to go and then he was home. Quickly he slipped through the entrance and disappeared down a sloping passage to his rooms. As soon as he got there he emptied his bags conscientiously in one of the new store-rooms. It was now almost full—a splendid sight!

Type 5

Paul Puffcheeks curled up comfortably in his bed-sitter to enjoy it and to recover from the exertions of his meeting with the lady hamster. It had simply demonstrated what he already knew: all the animals round here were emotionally wrapped up in themselves and blew up their trivial little feelings into huge problems.

Thank goodness he was above them in that respect; mentally he was on a much higher plane than all of them, and was not dependent on any relationship.

With satisfaction he contemplated his stores—stores which in fact he didn't need at all, but then on the other hand he did need them...

...but he preferred not to think any more about that just at present.

Type 5

(ii)
All Theories Yield to Love

HIGH UP in the old oak tree, next to the first fork in the branches on the left and from there right up at the very top, was the residence of Louisa the Owl. It was a little hollow in the tree-trunk, just big enough for one owl to fit into—but nothing else.

It was exactly the right size for Louisa, for there she could be all on her own, and at the same time feel wonderfully protected on all sides—like being in an egg. With the one difference of course that from an egg she would not have had such a magnificent view of the whole wood.

Louisa left her house only when it was strictly necessary. What she loved more than anything was to sit in her hollow, day and night, looking down into the wood or meditating. This was how she could best give free rein to her thoughts. And when Louisa gave her thoughts free rein the results were very unusual.

Just now, for example, she was busy pondering on the hidden connection which subsisted between all things. Everything that she observed—animals and plants, drops of water, snowflakes and the stars in the sky—all were regulated in accordance with laws which applied to the whole of life. She had arrived at this conclusion by way of philosophical reflection.

Louisa had been reflecting on this theme for a long time. And because she was endowed with very acute intelligence, she had already, on the basis of her observations and her

Type 5

knowledge, constructed a definitive theory, namely: the Reductionist Circle Hypothesis.

The thinking behind this was very complicated—so complicated that I cannot reproduce it here. But grossly oversimplified it went something like this: Every living thing, when detached from its own specific properties, can be ultimately traced to the geometric figure corresponding to the physical motion of the circle, and indeed from every point of view—the organic, the sociological and the metaphysical; or mathematically formulated: $\sqrt{DNS + H_2O + E}$—$y = (2r \cdot \pi)^3$

Whenever Louisa was able to discern the Reductionist Circle Hypothesis behind her observations, she felt it as a personal confirmation. For then she had managed to reduce the frightening multiplicity of the world in which she lived to a rational and comprehensible common denominator.

Her theory had also helped Louisa to cultivate a hobby which no other animal in the wood shared with her: she collected everything that was round. Every inch of space in her hollow that was not filled by her own person was crammed with circular objects: circular blossoms, snail shells, discs of bark and twig and much besides. Louisa devoted everything to her hobby. She even left her dwelling now and then to look for new objects to build up her collection.

And that was what she had planned to do this evening. She was already perched on the branch before her hollow and about to fly off when her glance lighted on the tree opposite hers, and she froze on the spot. For what she saw made her heart beat louder and faster. On a branch at the same height as her house a great barn-owl sat gazing at her steadily. He was a fine figure of a bird, intelligent-looking, and his eyes were the most perfect circles she had ever seen.

Louisa gazed back fascinated. A strange feeling rose in her, a feeling such as she had never known before. Obviously

Type 5

what was happening now suggested a completely new experience. Somewhat restless, she fidgeted about on her branch, and meanwhile observed herself as if from outside in order to analyse the effect this bird was having on her as objectively as possible.

She was a aware of a pleasant prickling sensation, and the skin under her feathers contracted with excitement. These symptoms could only have their origin in the intellectual challenge which sat facing her in bodily form. Mentally she gave the variable y its iterative value, calculated the formula and realized that this creature presented the most interesting confirmation of the Reductionist Circle Hypothesis she had ever seen.

The barn-owl continued to stare at her. Suddenly he spread his wings and left his tree. 'He's coming over here!' thought Louisa in dismay and flew off immediately to begin her search for new items for her collection—which had been her intention all along.

When she returned late at night the barn-owl was no longer there. Louisa sighed with relief. She didn't like other creatures to get too close to her. Although, in a way, she had rather hoped she might see the barn-owl again. That was illogical. Why was she being so illogical? Slightly confused, Louisa dropped into her hollow, shut her eyes and gave the matter serious thought.

But none of the theories and formulae which she had hitherto regarded as furnishing an explanation of life would work with this problem. Louisa was profoundly shaken. Nothing that had ever happened to her before had gone on puzzling her like this. And the worst of it was, this puzzle wasn't about something of no consequence; it meant that she no longer understood herself.

In the following days Louisa left her home more often than ever before. She collected circular objects, although there was

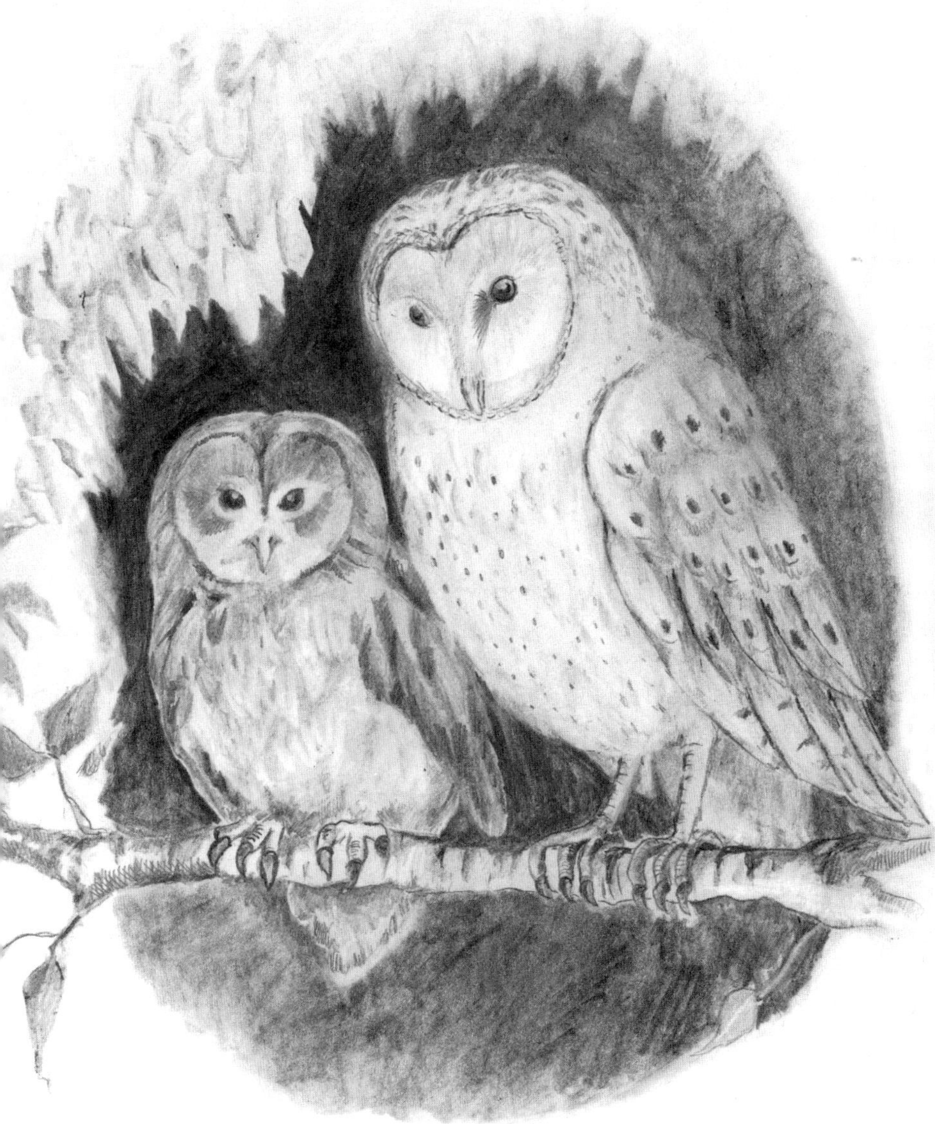

Type 5

no more room for them in her hollow, and hunted mice even when she wasn't hungry. She availed herself of every distraction.

Anything rather than think about the puzzle! Because whenever she sat down to think about it, or to meditate as she used to do, a strange feeling possessed her which she could in no way analyse to her satisfaction.

And then came a day when the barn-owl returned. One evening Louisa saw him again perched on a bough of the tree opposite. With his great eyes he was contemplating the full moon as it rose and he looked somehow very lonely and very sad.

And all of a sudden Louisa knew what this feeling meant: She was in love!

At first she was shocked and crept back as far as she could get into her hollow. But when the barn-owl was sitting in the tree again the next night and the night after that, then for a whole week and finally for a whole month, night after night, gazing sadly before him, Louisa saw that she must do something. For her inclination for him was growing ever stronger.

And so she gave herself a shake. She left her hollow, flew across to the barn-owl, sat down beside him and said: 'Good evening'.

Type Six

(i)

New Situations Create New Problems

THE WORLD of Conrad and his brother Otto consisted of a floor surface of 80 x 30 cms (20 mouse steps long x 8 mouse steps wide) and an exercise-wheel on which they could walk for as long as they liked without ever getting anywhere. It was a limited world, certainly, but a safe and manageable one.

One day however this world acquired, in the most literal sense, a hole. It was the day when the human beings had forgotten to shut the door of their cage.

Conrad was actually gnawing the plastic wall of the cage and complaining about its narrowness and the lack of freedom when he discovered it, and for a moment he couldn't believe his eyes. The doorway to freedom was standing open before him. All he had to do was to go through! He looked round at his brother for help. Otto was in the feeding-tray, tranquilly eating sunflower seeds. Clearly he had not yet noticed that the little door was standing open.

'Otto,' squeaked Conrad in a voice that trembled quite as much as his whiskers. 'Otto, look!' Otto looked up and followed the direction of Conrad's gaze. Baffled, he contemplated the open door of the cage. After some time he ventured timidly out of the feeding-tray and, sniffing cautiously, slowly approached the opening. Like his brother he didn't know what to make of it. For it was a new situation—and new situations are a problem because they usually require decisions.

Type 6

Conrad sat up on his hind paws and looked at his brother uncertainly. 'What shall we do?' he asked. Otto happened to be the elder of the two and when there was a decision to be made Conrad normally expected Otto to make it. But in the present instance Otto also seemed to find it difficult, for he went on thinking for a long time before he replied.

'We've often wished something like this would happen, haven't we?' he began at length. 'We do find this cage too narrow and we've always wanted to break out and gain our freedom. Now we've got the chance to do it. I suggest we disappear before we have second thoughts.'

Conrad gave his brother a searching look. Did he really mean what he was saying? Or was he in fact less confident than he appeared? Break out of the cage just like that?—it was a scheme that required very careful consideration.

'Have you thought of the dangers there might be out there?' he asked Otto. 'Just think, we might meet a cat!'

Otto shuddered. 'Yes, that would be terrible,' he agreed.

It was suddenly clear to both mice that the cage was not only a prison, but also a protection from danger. And all at once neither of them knew any longer whether they liked being in the cage because it protected them, or whether they hated it because it was a prison. The situation was becoming complicated.

For a while they sat in silence by the open door and groomed themselves out of sheer nervousness. Outwardly they were quite calm. But their heads were spinning with thoughts of the most alarming possibilities.

A terrible fear suddenly darted through Conrad's mind. 'I think I know why the door has been left open,' he whispered. 'It's a trick to lure us out of here! Probably there's a cat waiting somewhere for us to show ourselves, and when we are outside, she'll pounce on us!'

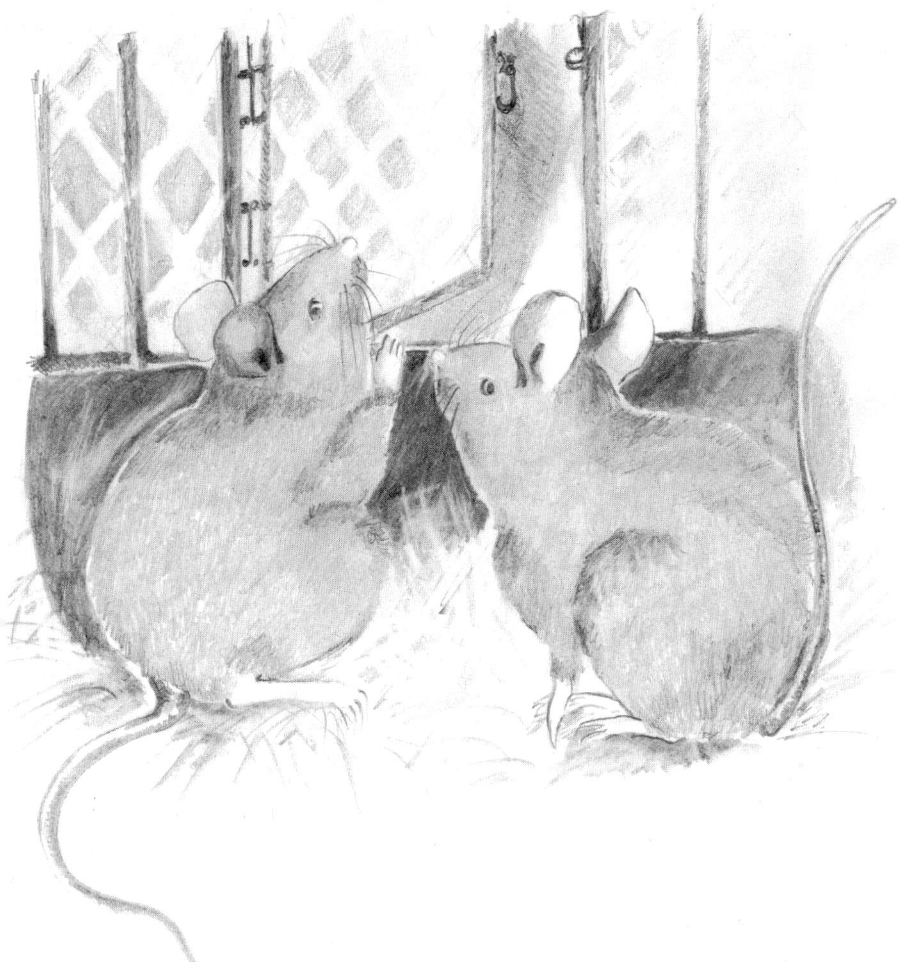

Type 6

At this moment the two mice heard a slight sound outside the cage. Conrad turned pale beneath his fur. 'The cat!' was all he could think—and like a flash he vanished into the farthest corner of the cage and hid under a pile of hay. There he remained lying motionless.

But Otto gazed as if hypnotised at the space between the bars. The uncertainty of not knowing what actually was out there was more than he could stand. And without really thinking what he was doing, he slipped through the door.

The world outside the cage was wide and empty and consisted, as far as Otto could tell, of nothing but brown carpet. By the time he had taken twenty-one mouse steps at the most, it was clear to him that this world was quite different from the one he had left behind. Even walking felt quite different here. That had nothing to do with the brown carpet, but it almost certainly arose from the fact that far and wide Otto could see nothing by which to orientate himself.

In the cage there wasn't infinite emptiness like this. In the cage there was a way from the sleeping-quarters to the feeding-tray, from the feeding-tray to the exercise-wheel, from the exercise-wheel to the water-bowl and from the water-bowl back to the sleeping-quarters. These ways were all familiar to him, even when he took them in a different order.

Slowly Otto began to wonder how he had ever come to think of the ordered and secure life in the cage as a prison. If this was what freedom looked like he didn't want anything to do with it.

Uncertainly he took a few more steps, and then he stayed where he was. His heart was beating fast. Twenty-five steps—he had never walked so far in his whole life. Except of course on the exercise-wheel. But that was different. On the wheel at least he didn't leave his familiar surroundings. Fearfully Otto looked round towards the cage. Then once

Type 6

more he heard a sound. At the same time he saw a gigantic shape advancing on him—and a hand coming down to seize him!

Otto was paralyzed with fear. He tried to run back but his feet were like lead. And in the next moment the hand had grasped him and put him right back where he belonged: in a world 20 mouse-steps long x 8 mouse-steps wide. With a slight squeak the little door of the cage closed behind him.

Cautiously Conrad came creeping out from under the hay. He sniffed his brother all over and Otto snuggled up to him. Softly squeaking and keeping close to each other they sat down in a sheltered corner of the cage. Conrad squeaked for joy at seeing his brother again, and Otto squeaked with relief at being back in his familiar surroundings.

Insecurity had vanished, the little door was closed again and the world was once more at rights.

Type 6

(ii)

The Brave Struggle with Fear

RUDOLF THE RABBIT was a handsome buck in the prime of life. He could run like the wind and was uncontested champion at 'doubling,' though he always modestly denied it. He lived with his wife Martha and their children in a cosy little burrow on the edge of the cornfield.

The tribe to which Rudolf belonged populated the whole area around the cornfield. It was very mindful of tradition and very large, for in accordance with the proverb among the rabbits, 'Big families mean security in old age', the does never produced less than eight young in each litter. Martha had just given birth to eight and the next litter was already on the way.

So Rudolf had good reason to be satisfied with life. However he did have worries—a few small worries and a lot of big ones. And sometimes he even suffered from acute anxiety. For life in these parts was full of dangers lurking everywhere and only waiting to overwhelm him at an unguarded moment.

True, he had never yet encountered danger face to face here on the edge of the cornfield, but that was just what made danger so dangerous! Just when everything looked so safe, when the birds were singing and the mice scampering carefree through the grass—that was when you had to be most on the alert and more cautious than ever.

Rudolf's greatest cause for concern at present however was his daughter Rosie. For Rosie went entirely her own way. She

Type 6

was a young rabbit who—to the dismay of her whole family—behaved completely differently from other rabbits. When all the rabbits in the warren smelt danger and fled for cover, Rosie would poke her impudent nose out of the burrow and snuffle inquisitively. When it was imperative to steal through the cornfield as inconspicuously as possible, you might be sure that Rosie would do all she could to attract attention. And when the Chief Rabbit issued instructions, Rosie made disrespectful remarks. Rosie even hopped on her own all the way to the farmyard, just to dance jigs in front of the dog-kennel, and if the cat were asleep, to pull her whiskers.

With her wild behaviour Rosie reduced the whole tribe to despair—and especially her parents.

Nor did her mother help matters by always appealing to her to respect time-honoured family tradition, to avoid dangerous situations and to fear enemies.

'Do remember,' she would preach at her several times a day, 'what your grandfather used to say: "Many fears are the rabbit's salvation!"'

'Pooh!—I have no fears,' was Rosie's reply to that, and one that she too came out with several times a day, waggling her ears skittishly. 'I don't give a buttercup for your middle-class morality.' And one evening she added: 'I'm going out!'

'But it's dark, it's raining, and it's extremely dangerous,' protested Rudolf in dismay. 'And where do you want to go anyway?'

'Tonight I'm going to sleep in the farmer's shed, right next to his fire-stick,' said Rosie cheekily, referring to the rifle which the farmer used for shooting any rabbits that came too near his kitchen garden. And the next moment she had vanished.

Rudolf, Martha and their children and a few other rabbits who had also heard these incredible words, their eyes big

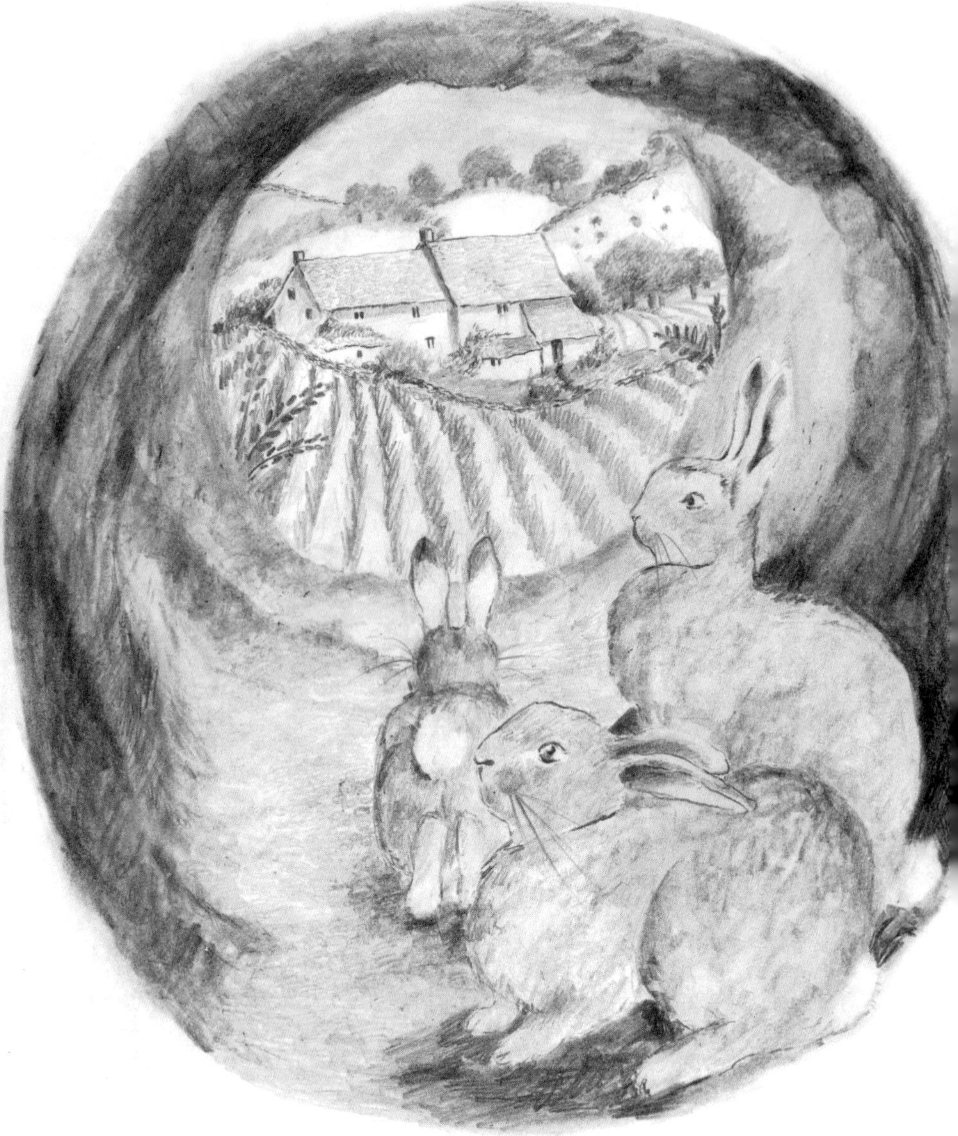

with fear, cowered quaking on the floor. Even to think about that rifle was intolerable, let alone talk about it. And now here was this young rabbit dashing recklessly to her own destruction!

But there was worse to come. In the middle of the night, as the rabbits sat huddled together in their burrow imagining all sorts of horrors, they heard a short, sharp report, followed immediately by another: the rifle!

In a flash the whole family was on Alarm Alert, which for rabbits means that they sat more silent and motionless than ever. Only their hind legs from time to time drummed on the ground to give the alarm signal to the other members of the tribe.

Again they heard the sound of gunfire. This time it was nearer than before. With quivering nostrils and ears laid back, the rabbits sat stiff with terror in their places. Not one of them dared to move. But thoughts were racing in Rudolf's head.

My daughter, Rudolf was thinking, she's out there and can't find her way back to us. And then came another thought: If she doesn't hurry she will entice the man here to the warren. And that will be the end—for all of us!

Rudolf pressed closer to the earth. His whole body trembled and his eyes rolled with terror. He was locked in a deathly struggle—the struggle against his instinct.

Another gunshot. The man must now be very near the cornfield. Then suddenly—at the moment of supreme danger—Rudolf's muscles lost their rigidity. He leapt up, cleared a way with his forelegs through his petrified family and sprang out of the protecting burrow. The smell of gunpowder made him feel faint with fear, but he forced himself to break cover and look out along the track through the field.

Type 6

Rosie was sitting in some bushes only a few yards away. She stared fascinated at the beam of light from the farmer's torch, searching for her. Rudolf guessed that she had lost her sense of direction. He had heard of this strange object that blinded you with its glare. With a single bound he was beside Rosie and bit her sharply in the ear. 'Run for your life!' Then he hopped a little way towards the farmer to catch his attention. The farmer shone his torch directly on to Rudolf and slowly raised his rifle. Rudolf shut his eyes to keep out the light and in a flash had doubled back across the field and vanished.

The man swore and fired after him, but as I've already said, Rudolf was a champion doubler. Not until he was sure that the farmer had given up the chase did he make a wide detour back to his family burrow.

The first thing he did was to pull the ears of his daughter Rosie—and among rabbits that is no laughing matter. Then he calmed down Martha who was still all of a tremble. And when the other rabbits in the warren had recovered from their fright, they praised Rudolf for his reckless daring and for his skill at doubling—which, as usual, he modestly denied.

Type Seven

(i)

Don't Burden Yourself with Negative Thinking

IN THE HEART of the Brazilian rain forest, in the topmost branches of the trees, lived the Schwips family. The Schwips family consisted of Father, Mother and three little Schwipses. And all three were so insatiably hungry for pleasure that they were almost like humans. Monkeys are often very like humans. Humans find that highly amusing and laugh at them.

'Kids,' shrieked Ma Schwips as she swung along from branch to branch, 'life's a treat! Everything you want is right under your nose. All ya gotta do is grab it!'

And with that she stuffed ten dates into her mouth at once.

'Yeah, Ma,' squealed the three little Schwipses, turning somersaults behind her. 'Life's a joke. We sure love it!' And they ripped coconuts, dates and peaches from the trees and what they couldn't eat they threw away. For the Schwipses lived on the fat of the land up there on the 'top floor,' and so they never even dreamt of coming down to earth.

Nearby on a thick branch sat Pa Schwips, cheerfully delousing himself. Pa Schwips fancied himself as a great thinker.

'Everyone gets from life exactly what he expects,' he informed the louse he had just picked out of his fur, and he gazed into its eyes. 'Every animal has the right to be healthy, successful and happy. So, the best of luck to *you*!'

And he tossed the louse in a wide arc over his shoulder and went to join his guzzling family

Type 7

Far below, on the 'ground floor' so to speak, Cora Crustycoat the Rattlesnake was gliding through the vegetation. Like all creatures who live close to the earth she had an acute sense of reality.

'What a load of nonsense,' she hissed, listening to the din overhead. Reality's nothing like that. Whatever you want you have to fight for—that's reality.' And her tongue flickered greedily in the direction of a young gazelle she had just espied feeding peacefully in the grass.

The Schwips family had meanwhile climbed out on the roof of the 'top floor'. All five stuck their heads out above the forest of leaves and enjoyed the wonderful view—a sea of green around them and over them the sun.

'It sure beats everything, up here,' cried Ma Schwips gaily.

'Our thinking gives form to the environment,' announced Pa Schwips. 'Creation is a mirror of our collective psyche—inwardly and outwardly.'

'What's that over there?' asked the smallest Schwips, pointing towards a black cloud of smoke rising from the trees not far away.

'Looks funny,' said Pa Schwips. 'Smells too, like someone's burnt their dinner.'

'M'mmm, smells like meat,' said Ma Schwips with a nervous laugh.

'Not monkey-meat, though,' her husband reassured her. 'Could be roast tiger, or baked sloth or maybe elephant steak. Hey, you know what one mouse said to the other when they were dining out? "The cooking in this restaurant ain't what it useta be. There's an elephant swimming in my soup!"'

The Schwipses shrieked with laughter, but it sounded a bit forced. 'Look,' cried the little Schwipses, 'that funny cloud's moving fast.'

'Yessir,' agreed Pa Schwips, 'and you all better do the same. It's sure moving faster than an ostrich.'

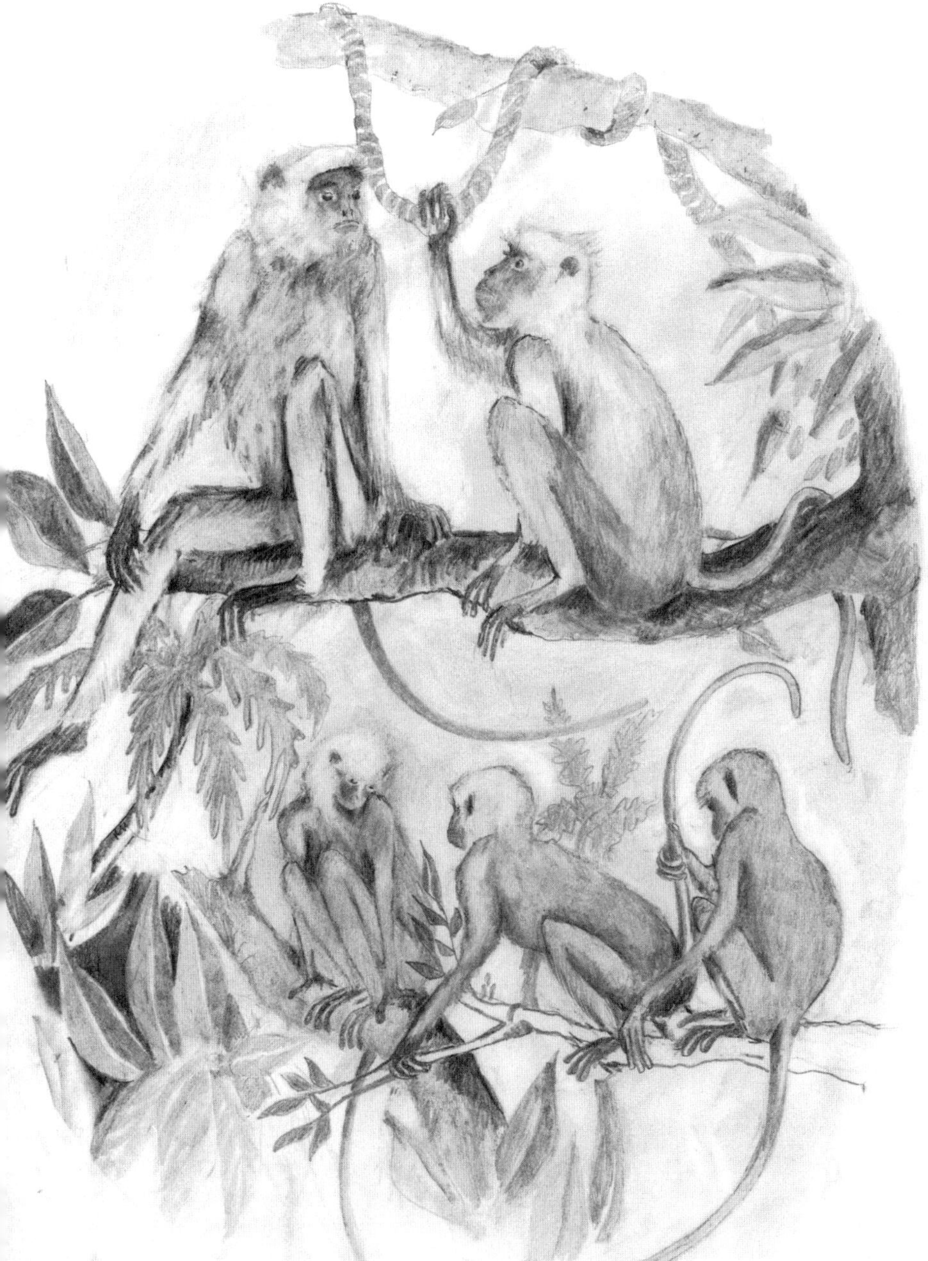

Type 7

On the ground below, Cora Crustycoat was worming her way towards the little gazelle, eager for the kill. Hearing the squeals of alarm on the 'top floor,' she stopped and listened. The young gazelle lifted her head too and sniffed the air timidly. Borne on the wind was the smell of fire, death and—human beings! An inner voice called to her: 'Flee!' And with a single bound she turned and leapt away through the undergrowth

Cora Crustycoat was also probing the strange smell in the wind with her flickering tongue. A fight was on, a life and death struggle! She would have to make for safety.

But first of all she wanted to leave her calling card for the humans. Her sense of justice demanded it. No one who destroyed the forest should go unpunished.

Cora Crustycoat opened her jaws to reveal long poisonous fangs. She could be very poisonous when she wanted. Her jaws rattling with rage, she slithered away through the vegetation—to the attack!

Meanwhile, up in the Schwipses' quarters, pandemonium reigned. All the animals were fleeing. It didn't matter where —anywhere away from the flames! But the flames were advancing rapidly. Was there any longer even a chance of escape?

Then Pa Schwips had an idea. 'Come on,' he yelled to his family, 'down to the river. If we dive under water we'll be okay.'

With loud shrieks the Schwips family now fled too. From a tall tree on the river bank Pa Schwips, Ma Schwips and the three little Schwipses all splashed into the cold water—just in the nick of time before the fire swept over them.

It was all over very quickly.

Type 7

What remained of the luxuriant forest looked like a desolate moonscape, with charred tree stumps standing up like ghosts under the blackened sky. The five Schwipses poked their heads out of the water and stared round in amazement.

Cora Crustycoat was emerging from the mud on the riverbank. She had a few burns on her stomach and looked pretty much the worse for wear, but she was quite satisfied. Before escaping into the river she had managed to deal out a few bites to the humans. That was life—give as good as you get.

When she saw Pa Schwips in the water she grinned maliciously. 'Well, how about your right to be healthy and happy and successful now?' she asked.

Cora Crustycoat not only had poisonous fangs, she had a spiteful tongue too.

'Don't know what you mean,' replied Pa Schwips. 'Sure, so a bit of the rainforest's been burnt down, but there's still plenty left.'

'So you don't reckon what's left might go up in smoke some day too?' asked Cora with a leer.

'My dear Mrs Crustycoat,' laughed Pa Schwips, 'that might not happen for years and years. We're living in the here and now, right? If you want to burden yourself with everything that might happen *some* day, you'll make your life a misery. Why not look on the bright side!'

'Old Shrunkskull,' hissed Cora Crustycoat testily, and she wriggled away. She sometimes showed a taste for colourful language.

Pa Schwips turned to lecture his family. 'Now there,' he said, 'you've got a good example of someone who makes herself downright disagreeable with negative thinking. So then: mind *you* always think positively. With the power of positive thinking you can shape yourselves and your lives.'

The little Schwipses were jubilant. 'Way to go, Pa!' they

Type 7
---

squealed. 'Think positive! Life is super-duper-mega-monkey-fun!' And they frisked and gambolled along behind their parents—through the burnt-out trees, on which not a single fruit hung any more.

Type 7

(ii)

Beneath the Surface of Life There Are Depths

A STRANGE object, wrapped in a thin gauzy web of fine-spun threads had been hanging for several weeks on the lilac bush in the back garden.

No one knew exactly what it was. Neither the garden inmates, nor the dog, nor the cat who lived indoors, and not even the stray tom-cat who now and then sauntered through the neighbourhood, and whenever he passed by the lilac bush tried to bring the thing to life with his paw.

Only the old owl, who had been observing the phenomenon for a long time, would have been able to tell them what it was. For one day, she had seen a little dust-covered caterpillar clamber on to the bush and take up its position on a branch where it remained motionless until it was completely covered in this strange filigree substance.

But the old owl kept her observation to herself. She was, after all, a reserved person.

One brilliant morning in June there were signs of movement in the queer thing on the lilac bush. The creature that was now forcing its way out of its wrappings looked quite different from the little caterpillar it had once been, as the owl, who again followed the whole process with close attention, observed with great interest. For this thing had wings—yellow wings that were still all stuck together and crumpled when it had at last completely emerged.

Type 7

The little insect clung to the lilac-bush and didn't seem to know what to do next. But after it had been sitting for a while in the sun, its wings unfolded of their own accord and it was a little butterfly who spread them and fluttered away.

Life seemed to it beautiful, easy and full of sunshine. It no longer thought of the time when it had crawled round as a caterpillar in the dust. Perhaps it had forgotten. Perhaps it simply didn't want to remember, for there was no pleasure in thinking about it.

Gaily and full of joy, it flew round the garden several times before alighting on one of the fragrant lilac blooms. Then it plunged its dainty proboscis into the delicious calyx.

'Are you pollinating here too?' inquired a bee who was going busily about her work a few flowers away.

'Pollinating—what's that?' asked the little yellow butterfly.

'There you are!' boasted another bee who was also working nearby, 'haven't I always told you? Butterflies are absolutely useless! They can't even pollinate!'

'He might learn how to,' rejoined the first bee. And turning to the butterfly she said: 'You have to be careful with your legs. The pollen will stick quite by itself if you just walk through the blossom in the right way. Yes, just as you're doing now. There, you've got it right first time!'

The little butterfly tried for a while to help with pollinating, but quite soon he got tired of it. He much preferred to fly about in the blue summer air and enjoy all the different flowers. So he left the lilac-bush and flew farther on.

In a shady spot by the back door lay the dog, a pedigree basset hound. He was deep in the melancholy contemplation of a rose-bush in full bloom, while his great ears trailed on the ground.

This was a sign of his breeding. Pedigree bassets are obliged to look like that, even when they are contemplating roses.

Type 7

As the butterfly fluttered down on to one of the roses the dog emerged from his profound reverie. 'Oh, what a fine colour composition!' he cried ecstatically. 'A yellow butterfly on a red flower—such vibrant colours...and yet doomed to die.'

And with these words he laid his head on his forepaws and looked sadder than ever.

'What do you mean "doomed to die"?' demanded the little butterfly. 'The sun is shining, the flowers are in bloom and we're alive!'

'In the midst of life we are in death,' murmured the basset sombrely. 'It's only the innocence of youth that doesn't see it.'

'Pooh, what a spoilsport you are!' grumbled the butterfly. 'Isn't there anyone in this whole garden I could have a bit of fun with?'

'You can have fun with me, little yellow fellow,' said a velvety voice, and a cat rubbed herself, purring, against the rose-bush where the butterfly was sitting.

'Let's play Catch,' she suggested. 'I'll sheathe my claws so as not to hurt you. Of course I could easily kill you,' she went on in a friendly tone, 'but I won't. And you'll be grateful to me for that ever after, won't you?'

'Oh yes—yes, of course,' stammered the little butterfly, rather taken aback.

Then he fluttered off and the cat tried to catch him.

At first the little creature felt a bit uneasy about this game, but then he began to enjoy it and went on playing until at last, tired out, he sank to the ground.

'That was great fun, but I've had enough for now,' he told the cat. 'Thank you for playing with me! You are the first really nice animal I've met in this garden.'

The cat purred with pleasure. 'You are a grateful little butterfly' she said. 'So let me give you a piece of advice: Look

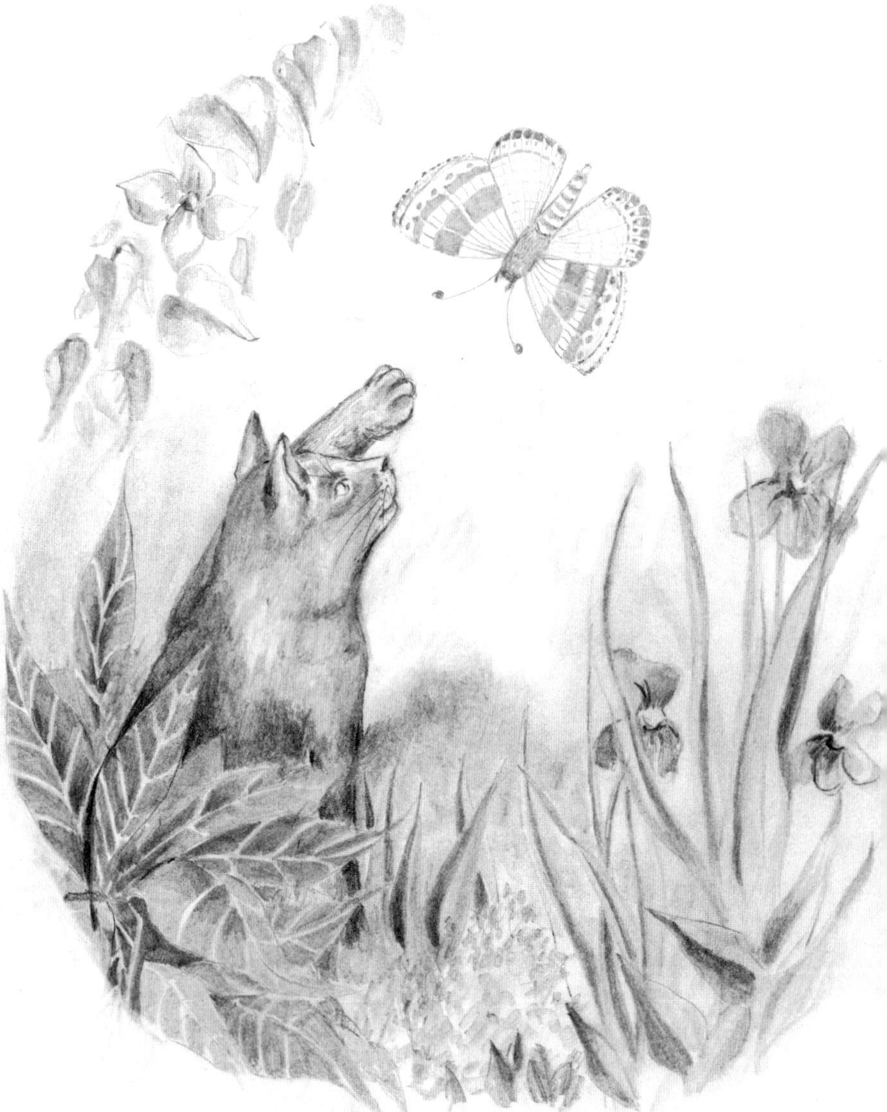

Type 7

out if you meet the stray cat! He will want to catch you, but he won't keep his claws in as I did. He might even kill you. He's a very crude, ruthless type, you see.'

'Kill me? How could anyone do a thing like that—on such a wonderful, warm, sunny day?' cried the butterfly as he flew high up again. 'All the same, thanks very much for the tip!'

Happily he frolicked through the air, drawn by their fragrance from one flower to the next and by the time he had reached the third flower he had already forgotten the cat's warning.

Gradually the day wore on to evening and all the flower-frequenting creatures began to seek their rest; only the little butterfly had not yet had his fill of flying. Intoxicated by the scent of the flowers, he was oblivious of the deepening darkness.

Nor did he see the stray cat who had begun his twilight patrol of the garden. And so the sudden blow of the great clawed paw took him completely unawares. All at once he was lying helpless on the ground, stunned with fear.

'Now we'll see what you're made of, you bit of yellow fluff,' snarled the cat. 'Either fight or make yourself scarce, but do something!'

Two dangerous green eyes and a whole row of sharp teeth loomed in front of the terrified butterfly. He flapped his wings and actually managed to get airborne. Panic-stricken, he fluttered away as fast as he could—anywhere away from there! On and on he flew deeper into the dusk until he got caught in the foliage of a tree and sat there utterly exhausted.

'So, there you are,' said the old owl. 'I've been waiting for you.'

The butterfly looked round startled. 'Who are you?' he asked. 'And how did you know I was coming? And why were you waiting for me?'

Type 7

'That's three questions all at once,' said the owl, perching where the butterfly could see her. 'I am the owl and nearly all the creatures come my way sooner or later. In your case, I knew you hadn't yet completed your cycle, and that's why I was expecting you.'

'I don't know what you mean...' stammered the butterfly, quite bemused.

'You don't have to,' answered the owl. 'It's a truth which exists quite independent of whether you understand it or not.'

Both were silent for a while. And then, all at once, the butterfly began to cry.

'Can you tell me why there is so much pain and wickedness in life?' he asked between sobs. 'Everything looked so lovely and so easy in the beginning. I thought that being alive meant being happy!'

The owl reflected for a moment.

'So it does,' she said at last. 'But only people who know what it is to suffer can be really happy. And only people who have experienced death know what life is. You yourself woke up to life so happy only because you had already died. You've forgotten, that's all.'

And the owl told the butterfly everything she knew about his past.

And so, with a great deal to think about, the butterfly flew back to the lilac-bush. He began to suspect that there were depths hidden beneath the surface of life—and he wanted to uncover them.

Type Eight

(i)
A Soft Heart Under a Thick Skin

NORBERT was a rhinoceros, and proud of it.

His thick hide, furrowed with scars, bore witness to many a bloody battle in which he had fought, and his over-worked horn sat askew, like a prize-fighter's nose. It was the third of its kind. Norbert had already lost a couple of horns in battle but fortunately they always grew again.

Norbert's territory was the savannah, and most particularly the area around the water-hole. And everybody had to respect that—or take the consequences.

Anyone who did venture onto Norbert's territory without permission had to be prepared either to be gored or at the very least driven off. For Norbert detested people who took liberties they had no right to take. But anyone approaching his frontier and asking politely if they might proceed further would be chased, beaten up or trampled. Norbert had an even stronger dislike of people who sidled meekly through life with no guts in their bellies.

In short, Norbert despised and disliked everyone who was not like himself. Basically he was the only person he knew whom he could respect.

It was the dry season in the savannah. Heat shimmered on the parched grass and Norbert lay asleep in his water-hole, which by now was no more than a muddy puddle. He always slept when he was not actually fighting. Strictly speaking, these were the only two activities with which he was familiar.

Type 8

Suddenly he was roused by a noise, a very slight one, but Norbert's hearing was excellent. So it didn't take him long to tell that it came from his stamping-ground.

Snorting with rage, he heaved himself out of the mud and looked round angrily in search of the enemy. But his eyes were not nearly as good as his ears. Actually, Norbert had always had a lot of trouble with his eyes, even as a youngster. He was, in fact, extremely short-sighted and saw everything only in black and white.

But that didn't deter him from charging with lowered horn in the direction from which the noise had come. Norbert came on at full tilt and the savannah shook under his feet, although the mere sight of him would have been enough to send any intruder running for his life.

But the enemy hiding there in the tall grass—whatever kind of a creature it was—made no attempt to flee, even with Norbert charging it like an enraged steam-engine.

Norbert braked within inches of the spot where he guessed the intruder to be hiding and stopped so abruptly that he sent up a thick cloud of dust. He wanted at least to have a good look at this reckless idiot before trampling it to death. But Norbert had to strain his eyes to see anything at all, so small was the creature in front of him.

It was a little bird, not half the size of Norbert's horn, and it seemed to be injured. Its left wing was spread at a curious angle, a thin trail of blood marked its progress over the boundary of the stamping-ground. As Norbert's gigantic face, which from the perspective of the little bird must have looked like a mountain range, loomed in front of it, it cowered deeper into the grass and chirped piteously.

Clumsily Norbert tramped all round the little bird, trying to get a good look at it from every side. And as he did so he stamped vigorously and tore up whole sods of earth with his horn, just for something to do. He had to do something so as

Type 8

to avoid having to admit that he really didn't know how to handle this situation.

The little bird sat terrified between Norbert's colossal feet and the long pointed horn ploughing up the earth around it. 'Please, do tread on me properly,' it chirped as loudly as it could. 'Then it will be over and done with!'

At these words a glimmer of recognition dawned inside Norbert. The creature before him was certainly minute, weak and injured but it seemed to be almost as brave in the face of death as a rhinoceros. That interested him. And—damn it all—he couldn't help somehow liking the little twit. It was so utterly unlike himself.

Norbert stooped right down into the grass and did his best to look the tiny thing straight in the face. 'Why the hell d'you want me to tread on you?' he asked, trying to make his voice sound mild and friendly, but it still came out like a growl of thunder.

The little bird was trembling. 'Because I can't survive with a damaged wing,' it replied. 'If I can't fly any more I'm as good as dead. It's the law of the savannah.'

Norbert drew himself up. 'There's only one feller makes the laws around here, and that's me!' he bellowed, glad that his moment of unwonted weakness was over and he once again had something to bellow about.

The little bird was practically blown away by Norbert's speech and flapped its sound wing. 'I can't do anything about it!' it twittered in despair. 'Sooner or later the hyenas will get me and then I'll be eaten!'

'Oh yeah? We'll see about that!' roared Norbert in a fury. 'I'll be damned if those lily-livered bastards get a feather off you!' Norbert's language was sometimes rather crude.

The little bird didn't know what was happening to him. As if by a gigantic excavator he was carefully scooped up on to Norbert's horn and carried off.

Type 8

Norbert had never made his way to the water-hole with such care. And as he put one foot cautiously in front of the other, holding his head as erect as he possibly could, to keep the little bird from slipping off his nose, he had grudgingly to recognize that something in him had changed.

Without knowing how it had happened he had become inwardly softer and more sensitive somehow—the hell he had! Good job he had a thick skin to cover it! Not that he was ashamed in front of the other animals—no fear, he didn't give a damn what others thought of him. But he didn't want to lose his own self-respect.

And, just to square things, he roared out a few pretty ripe oaths over the savannah, for the benefit of animals in general and hyenas in particular.

Then, grunting contentedly, he sank into his mud bath. 'You can stay up there just as long as you like,' he told the little bird. 'You won't have a thing to worry about and I can always keep an eye on you'.

'Thank you,' chirped the little bird timidly, as it caught a fat beetle that was crawling along Norbert's horn. 'Is it all right if I help myself up here?' Norbert grinned from ear to ear. 'Eat 'em all up,' he growled happily. 'Suits me fine.' And he closed his eyes and fell blissfully asleep.

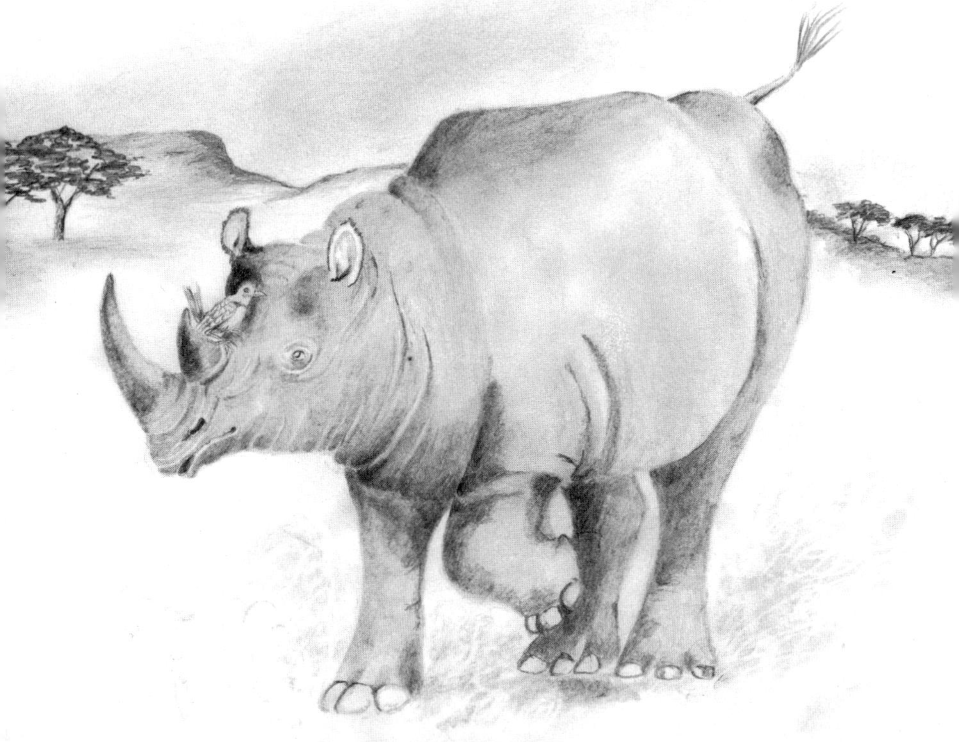

Type 8

(ii)
Might is Right

RANJIV KHAN a magnificent royal tiger and absolute overlord of the Indian jungle, rested in the noonday heat in the shade of a bamboo thicket and dictated a new Jungle Law.

Two little rhesus monkeys sat near him, at a safe distance. They waited respectfully for the words of the Khan before transcribing them with pointed sticks onto a large banana leaf. For all the animals had to submit to the dictates of their overlord and it was therefore important to write them down.

Truth and justice had hitherto attended the regime of Ranjiv Khan and they would continue to do so. But there were certain ordinances of the old Jungle Law which for some time Ranjiv had felt as restrictions on his own personal freedom.

Of course he himself would have thought nothing of simply overriding these rules, but his wife, the ravishingly beautiful tigress Sita, was of the opinion that the royal family should set an example and ought therefore to be subject to the law. And for her sake he intended in future to abide by it. But first of all it would have to be changed in certain respects.

'Jungle Law: Paragraph I,' roared Ranjiv, and the two little monkeys ducked their heads in fright and began to write. 'Paragraph I as follows: *Anyone who is up to it is permitted to have several wives simultaneously.*

The monkeys nudged each other and tittered. That was

Type 8

unwise, for if the Khan had noticed he would have gobbled them both up without further ado and sent for fresh clerks. But Ranjiv took no notice of them.

Just then, in fact, he was purring over the thought of his romance with Ravna, the beautiful black panther. Ranjiv Khan loved exotic women—especially when they were as tempestuous as Ravna. Sita knew about this affair; she had smelt Ravna's perfume on the royal fur and had promptly made a scene.

Ranjiv Khan stroked his mighty whiskers in some amusement. She had a lot of temperament, his little Sita. But who could stop him, Ranjiv Khan, from doing something that was forbidden? Well—in future it would be forbidden no longer.

'Jungle Law Paragraph II,' he continued with a snarl, and both the little monkeys at once stopped giggling and bent assiduously over their banana leaf. *'Whoever has might has right on his side'*.

Ranjiv repeated this sentence for he found it remarkably fine. What a fantastic chap he was, to be able to turn out such a formula—just like that!

'Have you got that down?' he growled at the two rhesus monkeys, who at once nodded obediently.

Ranjiv surveyed them with contempt. These two brainless subjects certainly had no might, so they had no rights either. Later on he would have them for a midday snack. When they'd finished writing, of course.

He rolled over on his side, licked his paws and thought about the third paragraph.

Meanwhile his secretaries were playing Catch in the bamboo thicket or hitting each other in turn with the banana leaf amid shrieks of merriment—until Ranjiv sprang into their midst with a single bound.

'You're here to work, not play,' he roared furiously.

Type 8

'Yes, great Khan,' whispered the monkeys, trembling, as they scuttled to the ground with their banana leaf and seized their writing-sticks.

The great tiger lay down dangerously close to them in the grass and fixed them with his blazing green eyes. 'Paragraph III as follows: *All animals are either winners or losers. The losers are there to be eaten by the winners.*'

The two monkeys gulped, their writing implements dropped from their hands.

'Well then, get a move on!' commanded Ranjiv Khan and his tail thrashed the ground.

'Your Highness,' whispered one of the monkeys, greatly daring, 'permit me to observe that such a decree is not just. Please have the goodness most graciously to amend this paragraph.'

The eyes of the tiger shone with a baleful gleam. 'Not *just*, did you say? A decree promulgated by me is not *just*?'

Frightened, the monkey retreated a step and raised its hands in pleading. 'I didn't mean it like that, great Khan—I only...'

But he got no further, for without delay Ranjiv Khan acted in accordance with Paragraph III of his own Law, and the monkey was eaten on the spot. The other one fled wailing into the jungle.

Only the banana leaf with the first two paragraphs of the new Jungle Law was left lying on the ground. With one blow from his paw Ranjiv sent it spinning into the undergrowth. Then he let out a great roar of rage, so loud that all the animals round about at once ran for cover, and finally he lay down again majestically in the grass.

To hell with the Law—why waste words on it? He did what he wanted and Sita would just have to make the best of it. What a stupid idea to change the Law because of Sita,

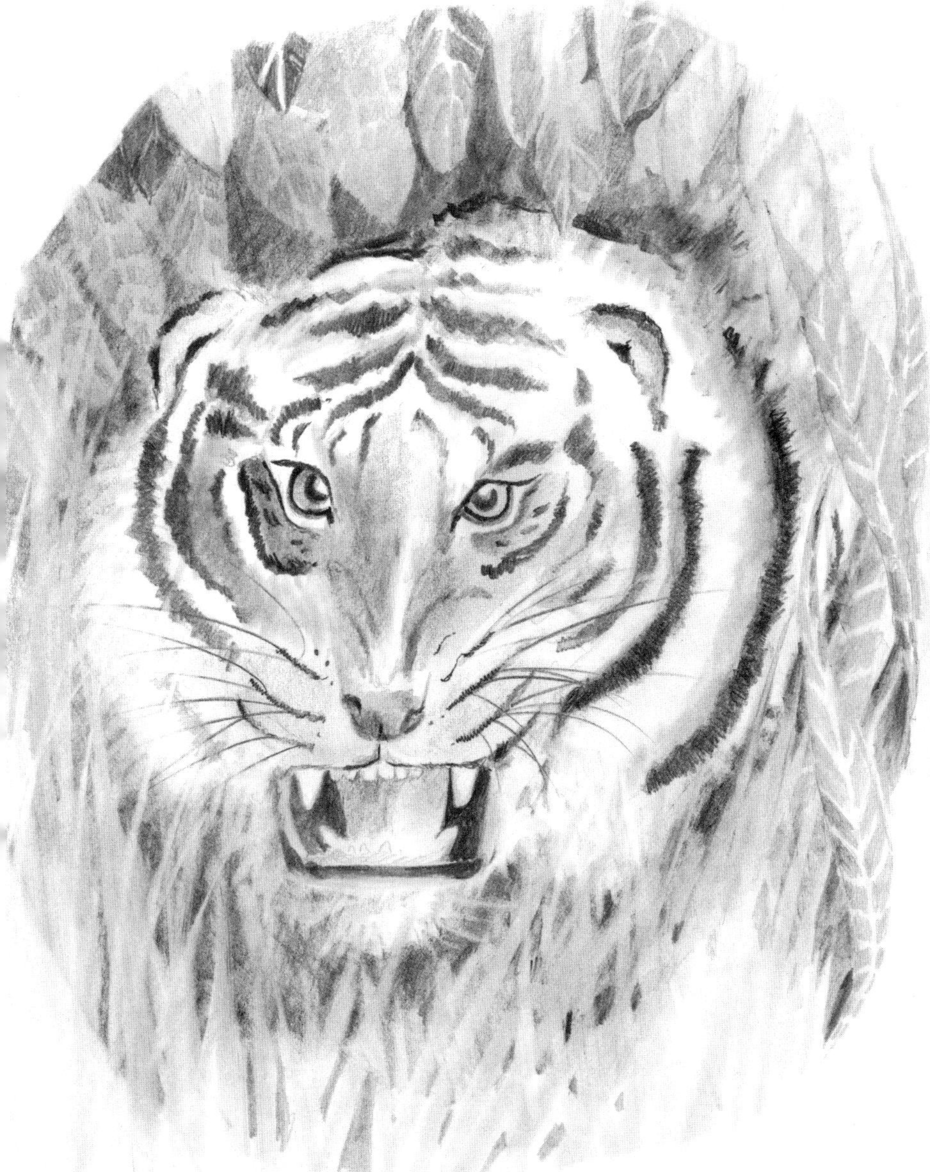

Type 8

so she wouldn't have to see how he flouted it. Flouting the Law was the very thing that made it such fun!

Now in a thoroughly good mood and very pleased with himself for deciding not to renounce that pleasure, he got up and stretched luxuriously.

The sun had set and the air was cooler now. Ranjiv Khan left the bamboo thicket and with sinuous movements stole into the jungle: time for the evening prowl; time to show himself to his subjects, their very own overlord, powerful, virtuous and just.

Type Nine

(i)

Anything for Peace and Quiet

THE SUN was rising over the treetops of the forest. Pedro the Sloth, who, as usual, had been hanging all night from his favourite branch in his sleeping-tree, blinked lazily in the morning light and asked himself, as he did every morning, whether he should wake up now or go to sleep again.

After considerable reflection Pedro decided against waking up. He was hanging so comfortably at the moment. There were still about six or eight hours to go before siesta, so it was worth sleeping half way round the clock.

He was just about to close his eyes again when the tree was shaken from its roots to its crown by a tremendous creaking noise: the tree-trunk had sloped sideways. For a long time termites had been eating it away.

Birds flew up, monkeys fled screeching onto the nearest trees, and although Pedro went on hanging there he was badly frightened. His sleeping-tree was under threat!

If the termites carried on like this it would soon crash. Slowly it dawned on Pedro that he would have to do something, even though he loathed the idea because it would ruin his peace and quiet. Besides he had no idea what to do. He'd got to do something or other. But what?

The sun was already higher in the sky by the time Pedro had reached a decision: he would look for a new sleeping-tree. Or would it perhaps be better to ask the termites to leave his tree alone?

Type 9

No, better not. It might lead to a confrontation, even an argument, and that he must avoid at all costs. Probably it would be the best thing to look for a new sleeping-tree. It shouldn't be all that difficult, there were plenty of trees in the forest after all. But he would have to hurry if he wanted to be finished in time for siesta.

Sluggishly Pedro opened his eyes, still gummed with sleep, and looked round wearily for the nearest branch from which he could dangle. Having located the branch and worked out the way to get down to it, he decided it really was time now to begin his search. First of all though he would like something to eat.

Pedro knew where to find the juiciest leaves on this tree: right at the very top, not far from his sleeping place. It was several months since he had been up there. He didn't often make the exhausting and troublesome ascent, mostly contenting himself with the leaves that grew farther down. But today he felt the need of something specially nice.

Pedro proceeded in slow motion, branch by branch up the tree, but the sun was getting rapidly higher in the sky. Halfway up he had to stop, exhausted and sweating from the heat.

Drained of energy, he took a rest and gazed dreamily out over the forest. From here he had a wonderful view. An ocean of green foliage and brilliant flowers waved far below him. Dazzling birds and glittering insects flew over it and he could hear somewhere under the trees the babbling of a little stream. The sun was reflected in its clear water and Pedro saw little sparkles between the green leaves.

At this point he realized how thirsty he was! In this heat he definitely needed a drink of water from that lovely refreshing cold stream That would soon liven him up! In imagination he

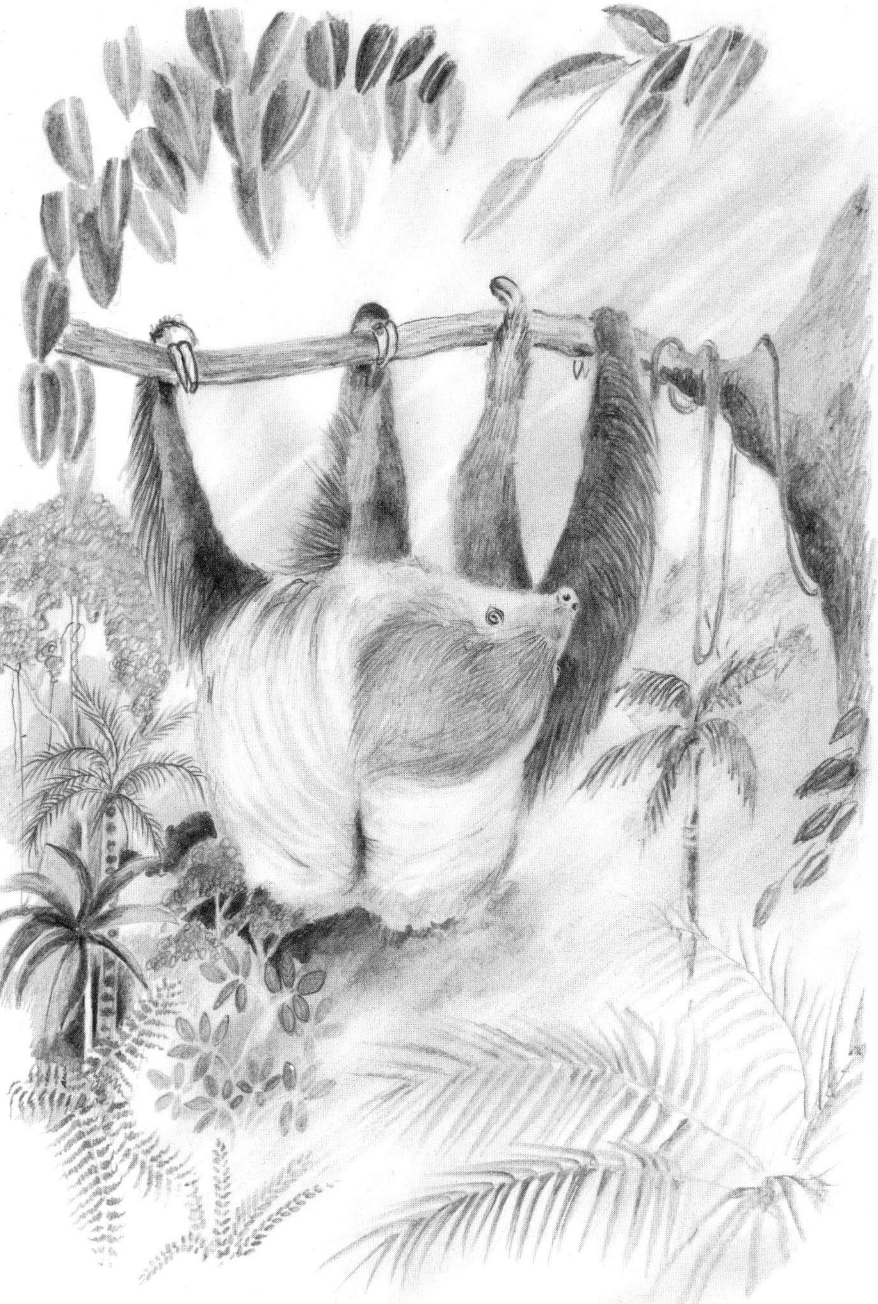

Type 9

could already feel the cold water running down his throat and it made him thirstier than ever.

So he prepared himself for the descent. A last look to judge the distance showed him that he still had a good way to scramble down to the bottom. Fortunately, going down always used less energy than going up. Pedro relaxed his grip and felt for the nearest branch. Cautiously and very slowly—one hand after the other, one foot after the other—he made the descent.

The sun stood pitilessly high and when Pedro passed his sleeping-place on the way down it was already midday.

Pedro had just stopped to hang on the next-best branch and pause for recovery when he saw it: The sun was directly over him. Siesta! What a good thing his sleeping-place was so near! Why on earth had he been clambering around all that time in the tree? Ah well, never mind—he was here again and that was all that mattered.

With a sigh of satisfaction, Pedro took hold of his favourite branch, draped himself around it and at once fell asleep.

Type 9

(ii)

It Does One Good to Speak One's Mind

**Indian Elephant
Native Land: Malaysia
*Please do not feed!***

THIS NOTICE stood in front of the enclosure in which for many years Samadhi the Peaceable had carried out his well-regulated duties.

His work suited him and even when it was strenuous he enjoyed doing it. Each day when the zoo opened he was standing behind the ditch surrounding his enclosure, flapping his ears benevolently, affably extending his trunk this way and that, and from time to time emitting a trumpet-blast.

He worked eight hours a day and his working day cost him a lot of strength. For Samadhi the Peaceable had to make a great effort to suppress his latent energy. With such a quiet occupation as his there was no alternative.

Obviously the continual output of strength made him very tired, and so it was quite natural that he should find it necessary to interrupt his work every now and then for a little snooze. He would seek out an undisturbed spot behind the rocks, tuck his mighty elephant legs under him and let himself float on the sounds all around him as if on a wave.

In his dreams he leapt with the gazelles, prowled with the tigers, climbed with the monkeys and soared with the eagles.

Type 9

In his dreams boundaries dissolved, contrasts vanished. Mystical was the Unity binding all living things and contentment was her gift to all who dwelt in her.

Outside on the path Magnus Finefeather the Peacock, professional advertising consultant, was strutting past the elephant enclosure. Complacently he showed off his tail feathers and turned proudly this way and that in front of the whirring and clicking cameras.

'What you need for your job,' he told Samadhi the Peaceable, 'is an appropriate logo, a symbol of your own that can't be mistaken for anyone else's.'

Samadhi the Peaceable blinked good-naturedly. 'Is that important?' he asked. 'Nothing is really important in this world, you know, and all endeavours are transient. I am content with my work just as it is. Modesty—as my Mother used to tell me, peace be to her soul—let modesty be the pearl for which you strive, and...'

'An effective advertising symbol is indispensable for publicity,' interrupted Magnus Finefeather unperturbed, as he twirled round officiously in front of the enclosure. 'Of course it wouldn't need to have the same elaborate finish as the one I've got,' and he fanned out a particularly brilliant wheel. 'There are other possibilities. For your purposes, I could imagine for instance a knot in your trunk or something of that sort. If you're interested I would be very happy to advise you on detail.'

But Samadhi the Peaceable was not the slightest bit interested. What interested him at the moment was the zookeeper, who—praised be his diligent hands—was bringing the elephant feed. Appetising was the fare in this zoo, and pleasant it was to receive it with an expectant trunk.

Type 9

In another enclosure, the one next to Samadhi the Peaceable, lived Phoebe Fleetfoot the Gazelle, a specialist in all matters of security. 'As if there were no more urgent problems in the world than getting yourself logos and suchlike,' she said. 'We've all got enough to do with looking after our security. There are so many risks in life these days!'

Samadhi the Peaceable gave her a friendly nod. He was not able to answer her at that moment because he happened to be stuffing a large helping of hay into his mouth with his trunk.

'There are dangers lurking everywhere. I'm sure you know that as well as I do,' continued Phoebe Fleetfoot. 'You must already be aware that in every bite of hay you take there may be—forgive me for me for speaking so frankly—a mouse hiding.'

Samadhi the Peaceable choked and began to cough violently.

'See! It can happen like that—in a flash!' cried Phoebe Fleetfoot in triumph. 'You simply cannot be too careful. But I do apologise,' she went on diffidently, drawing back a few steps from the fence, 'perhaps I've projected something negative into your feeding pattern? Maybe I got too close to you? I'm very sorry if I did.'

Samadhi the Peaceable refrained from uttering the not very flattering words that were on the tip of his tongue. It was always less exhausting to suppress an impulse than to let things build up into an argument. So he confined his answer to a glazed look and a wide yawn.

Tedious was the woman's chatter and wise indeed was he who ignored it. Deep in reverie he went to his usual haunt behind the rocks, tucked his elephant legs under him and dropped off for an after-dinner nap.

And life went on all around him. The rhinoceros over the way was churning up the sand in his enclosure; the tiger in

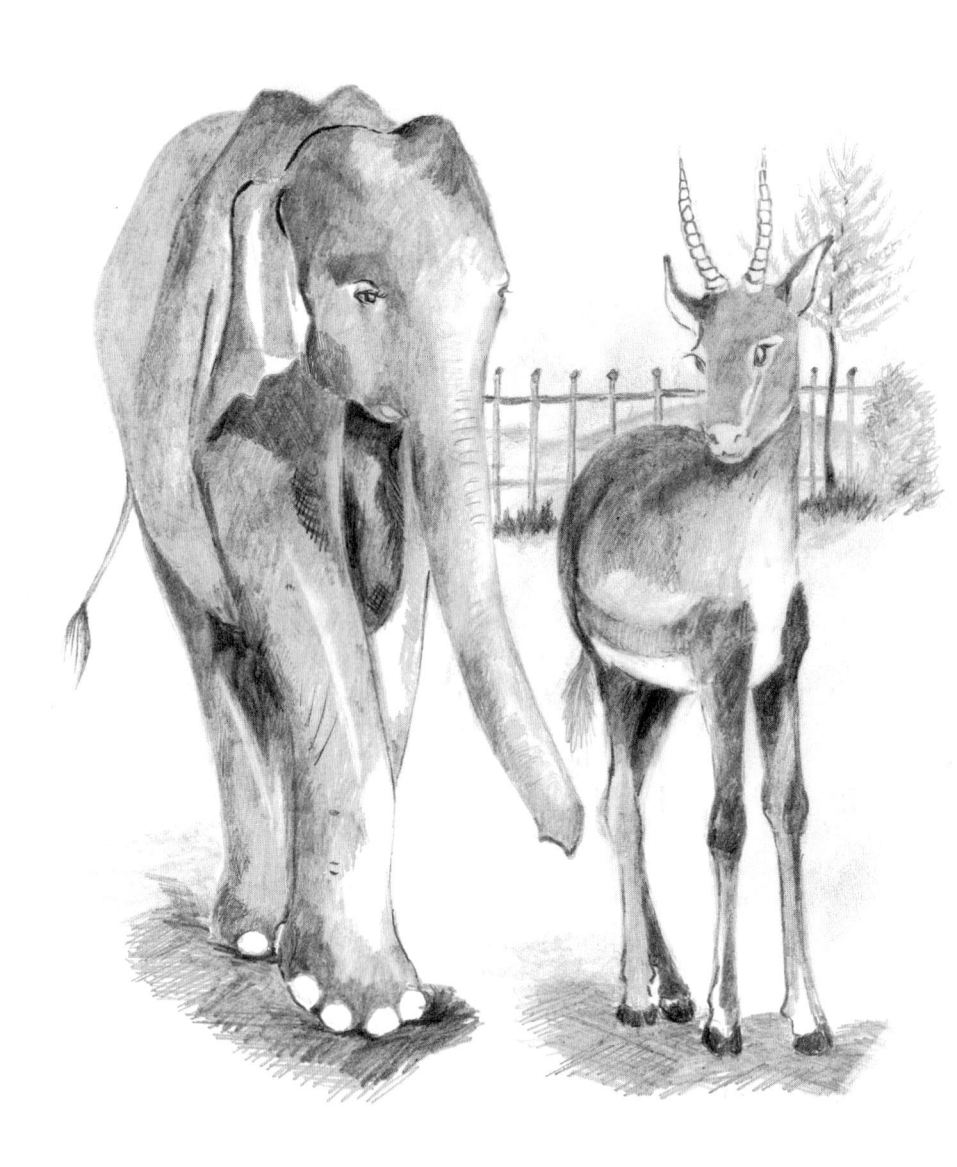

Type 9

the Big Cats' cage snarled angrily because he didn't like the rhinoceros; in the park pigeons sunned themselves, until a loudly yapping terrier chased and scattered them.

Two of the pigeons fluttered over to Samadhi's enclosure. 'Let's fly further on,' cooed one to the other. 'There's only a boring old elephant here'.

Samadhi the Peaceable sighed. In a way he could understand them all—without exception. But how exhausting was the multiplicity of creatures, and how wearisome the variety of beings! Sweet and delectable would true harmony be, and unity fragrant as the flowers of the Orient. Samadhi the Peaceable sighed yet again. Then he got heavily to his feet and went back to work.

At this moment a crowd of children ran past, all chattering merrily. It was a school outing. Their biology teacher, Miss Philomena Smallweed, followed the children a little way off and at a slower pace.

Samadhi the Peaceable was glad, for he loved children. So he waved his ears more playfully than ever and stretched his trunk even farther across the ditch.

When Miss Smallweed reached the enclosure, the children quietened down.

'Now this is an elephant,' explained Miss Smallweed in shrill tones. 'The elephant will grow to a height of four metres and has a long trunk.'

The children were all eyes and attention.

'Scientific research has shown,' Miss Smallweed continued, 'that the elephant is deficient in energy and its intellectual capacity is virtually nil. Furthermore, as you can see even from its bodily structure, it has a certain tendency to laziness.'

Little Fred was just putting up his hand to ask a question, when Samadhi the Peaceable drew himself up to his full

Type 9

height and, lifting his trunk before the eyes of the frightened class, blared out a mighty fanfare.

'I have no tendency to laziness nor is my intellectual capacity virtually nil,' he trumpeted, so loudly that the whole zoo could hear him. 'I am not a boring old elephant, and you, my dear Mrs Fleetfoot, have got on my nerves with your obsessive chatter about security. Nor do I need a logo, and a knot in my trunk would be an abomination. So now you all know!'

Samadhi the Peaceable took a deep breath. It had done him good to say that.

And peacefully he turned back again to his work, waving his ears benevolently and extending his trunk affably this way and that.

FURTHER READING

Baron, Renee and Wagele, Elizabeth, *The Enneagram Made Easy*, HarperSanFrancisco, 1994.

Beesing, Marian, Nogoesek, Robert J. and O'Leary, Patrick, *The Enneagram, A Journey of Self-Discovery*, Dimension Books, 1984.

Ebert, Andreas, and Küstenmacher, Marion, eds., *Experiencing the Enneagram*, Crossroad, 1992.

Metz, Barbara and Burchill, John, *The Enneagram and Prayer, Discovering Our True Selves Before God*, Dimension Books, 1987.

Palmer, Helen, *The Enneagram, Understanding Yourself and the Others in Your Life*, HarperSanFrancisco, 1991.

Rohr, Richard and Ebert, Andreas, *Discovering the Enneagram, An Ancient Tool for a New Spiritual Journey*, Crossroad, 1990.